Peck felt the presence before he saw it. The hairs on his neck stood out and his skin felt like it was covered with crawling insects. Some primal instinct told him to stop where he was, or better yet, turn and run.

"Stop it. There's nothing to be afraid of," he said out loud just to break the unnatural silence. He hadn't gone ten yards when a thing straight out of a bad acid trip stepped out of the woods and onto the road in front of him. He froze in place. What the hell is that? He knew instinctively it was not a man in a cos¬tume. This was the real thing … a Bigfoot.

If the one in the museum was scary, this one was terrifying. It was taller and more massive. It was at least eight feet tall and covered in coarse red fur. Its chest was wide and deep, its arms impossibly long, with hands the size of dinner plates. One of them could easily fit around his skull like his hand could grip a grapefruit.

They stood there on the road, neither one moving. Peck wanted to run, but he was frozen in place until the creature snarled and took a step toward him. When it threw back its head and roared, he saw long, yellowed canines that could rip an animal apart. Peck's bladder let go and a warm stream of urine ran down his leg and soaked into the costume that was already damp from sweat.

ALONE?

BY DAN FOLEY

PART ONE

THE CHALLENGE

ONE

Fraternity brother or not, Michael Peck hated Pierce Chambers. Chambers was everything he wasn't, and the guy knew it. He was blond with blue eyes, six feet tall with an athlete's body, and good-looking to boot. Girls loved him. Michael was five foot six inches tall with mouse brown hair and so thin he looked anemic. He had an acne-scarred face he tried to cover with a beard that never really filled in enough to hide anything.

Chambers never said anything disrespectful to Michael. He didn't have to. His eyes and self-satisfied smirk said it all. Michael wanted to punch that smirk off his face every time he saw it, but Chambers would beat the crap out of him if he ever tried it. He'd have to find another way to get back at him for the three years of anxiety Chambers had put him through. He still had another year of school left, but Chambers would be graduating at the end of this semester. It was now or never if he was going to get some payback. He just had no idea how to do it.

Here it comes, Peck thought, as he sat in the frat's living room as another installment of *Alone* came to a close. It was a fraternity favorite, but at the conclusion of every episode, Chambers invariably bragged, "I could so do that." And, sure enough, as soon as the credits started to roll, Chambers made his announcement. That's when inspiration struck. Michael knew exactly how he was going to shame the asshole.

Peck was in the living room the next time the show was on. He arrived a half hour before it started just to make sure he could be in Chambers' favorite chair, the comfortable recliner, when the prick got there. Chambers arrived ten minutes before show time, just like Michael knew he would. He looked up, but didn't say a word when Chambers saw him sitting in *his* chair. He was disappointed when all Chambers did was drop onto the aging, threadbare couch that should have been tossed out years ago. Still, it was a small victory and he'd take it.

That's alright, just wait, he thought as Chambers shifted around trying to get comfortable. Two more frat brothers, Derick Stanley and Pete Priolo, came in, forcing Chambers to share the couch.

Peck sat on pins and needles the entire show, waiting for Chambers to utter the inevitable "I could so do that." It never came. He was ready to storm out of the room, when, right at the end, Chambers said it. His pronouncement was met with the standard response from his fraternity brothers—a chorus of moans. That's when Michael hit him with it. "You ever think of putting your money where your mouth is, Chambers?" He didn't know whether the prick was more shocked at the challenge, or at Michael talking to him.

He thought Chambers was going to ignore him, but then Stanley, who disliked Chambers almost as much as Peck did, chimed in with, "Yeah, Chambers, what about it? You up for that?"

Chambers looked at them, smirked and answered, "Of course I'm up for that, but I'd never be able to get on one of those shows. You all know that."

"Yeah, but you'd do it if you had the chance, right?" Michael asked.

"Of course."

"Great, because I've got an idea. Why don't we all chip in and send you on an adventure of your own."

"What do you mean *'an adventure of my own'*?"

"Exactly that—an adventure of your own. Just like the ones on the show. We can all chip in enough to get the gear you'd need. We'll pick a site, drop you off and you can show us all you're not just a bullshit braggart. What do you say?"

Chambers wanted to say "Fuck you, Peck," but the smug look on Peck's face and the grins of some of his fellow "brothers" pissed him off. He felt a moment of doubt, but then blurted out, "Fine, you get the gear and I'll do it."

"No problem," Peck answered, and gave a thumbs up to the rest of the guys in the room.

It wasn't until later that night, as Pierce lay in his room listening to Steve Cusack snoring, that the seeds of doubt took root in his brain. It was easy to say he could do it … but could he? When he thought about how much a thing like that would cost, he went to sleep relieved knowing Peck could never pull it off.

When Pierce woke up the next morning, Cusack was still asleep, making noises like a freight train. On his way to the bathroom, he noticed three sheets of paper lying on the floor that someone must have slipped under the door sometime during the night. *What the hell are these*, he thought, as he bent to pick them up. He glanced at the first one and found a list of equipment someone, Peck no doubt, had copied from the *Alone* website on the History channel. It was a complete list of the equipment provided each contestant on the show. He tossed the papers on the bed, hardly glancing at them. He'd go over them in detail later that afternoon. Right now he was running late for a creative writing class.

"Hey Chambers, you getting cold feet yet?" someone yelled as he bolted out the door. He heard laughing before it slammed shut behind him.

Screw you guys, he thought, as he hurried off to class.

Calls of "Hey, Survivor Boy" and "Wilderness Man" greeted him when he came back to the frat house later that afternoon. There was even one "Yo, Grizzly Adams."

He ignored them all and retreated to his room, face burning, and wondering, *Who the hell is Grizzly Adams?* He threw his books on the bed and grabbed his computer. A quick search on the internet told him who Adams was, but it only added to his embarrassment … and anger. Then he turned his attention to the sheets with the equipment lists that had been stuffed under his door in the night.

The first page was a list of Clothing/Apparel/Personal Effects every contestant on the show gets. Prices had been added in red behind each item.

1 pair of high leg Hunting boots ($200)
2 pairs of outdoor pants (can unzip into shorts) ($60)
1 t-shirt ($5)
2 fleece or wool shirts (hooded or unhooded) ($280)
3 pairs of wool socks ($30)
1 hat (brimmed, wool or baseball) ($36)
1 bandana or shemagh ($3)
1 pair gloves ($80)
1 light outdoor jacket ($160)
2 pairs of underwear ($10)
1 rain jacket and rain trousers ($70)
1 thermal underwear (long) ($235)
1 pair of gaiters ($100)
1 pair of Crocs, Teva sandals or Keen sandals ($60)
1 toothbrush ($0)
1 pair of prescription eyeglasses (if needed)
1 personal photograph
Total = $1369

Next there was a list of Tracking/Safety equipment every-one gets:

2 safety tools (may consist of a canister of wild animal repellent, an air horn and/or 1 flare) ($50)
1 rules and regulation guide ($0)
1 backpack ($200)
1 camera pack ($100)
Camera equipment ($5000)
1 emergency flare ($10)
1 satellite phone ($2000)
1 emergency personal flotation device ($50)
1 first aid kit (military type – tourniquet, ace bandage, alcohol, plastic bag, etc.) ($20)
1 small mirror ($5)
1 20x20 canvas tarp ($30)
1 10x10 tarp for protecting camera and equipment ($20)
1 GPS tracking device ($350)
1 head lamp ($50)
1 emergency rations pack to include water and food etc. ($100 estimated)
Total = $7985

The final list consisted of personal items. It was the longest of the lists, but he would only be allowed to select ten items to take with him. No prices had been added to these items.

Shelter:
12x12 ground cloth/tarp
8mm climbing rope – 10m
550 paracord – 20m
1 hatchet
1 saw
1 axe

Bedding:
1 multi-seasonal sleeping bag fitted to provided backpack
1 bivy bag (Gore-Tex sleeping bag cover)
1 sleeping pad
1 hammock

Cooking:
1 large (no more than 2-quart) pot, includes lid
1 steel frying pan
1 flint or ferro rod set
1 enamel bowl for eating
1 spoon
1 canteen or water bottle
1 bear canister

Hygiene:
1 bar soap
1 8 oz tube of toothpaste
1 face flannel
1 40m roll of dental floss
1 small bottle bio shower soap
1 shaving razor (and 1 blade)
1 towel (30" x 60")
1 comb

Hunting:
1 300-yard roll of nylon single filament fishing line and 25 assorted hooks (no lures)
1 primitive bow with 6 arrows (must be predominately made of wood)
1 small gauge gill net (8m x 2m OR 1.5m deep x 3.6m long and 2" [50 mm] mesh)
1 slingshot/catapult
1 net foraging bag
1 3.5m roll of trapping wire

Food:
5 lbs of beef jerky (protein)
5 lbs of dried pulses/legumes/lentils mix (starch and carbs)
5 lbs of biltong (protein)
5 lbs of hard tack military biscuits (carbs/sugars)
5 lbs of chocolate (simple/complex sugars)
5 lbs of pemmican (traditional trail food made from fat and proteins)
5 lbs of gorp (raisins, M&M's and peanuts)
5 lbs of flour (starch/carbs)
2 lbs of rice/ 2 lbs of sugar / 1 lb of salt

Tools:
1 pocket knife
1 hunting knife
1 Leatherman multi-tool
1 sharpening stone
1 roll of duct tape or 1 roll of electrical tape
1 small shovel
1 small sewing kit
1 LED flashlight
1 pair of ice spikes

The list was an eye-opener. He had never really thought about what was needed for an extended stay in the wilderness. More than that, he had never seriously thought about what the contestants *didn't* get. There was a list of prohibited items, but basically, if it wasn't already listed, it was prohibited.

Damn! This thing is getting out of control. Someone, it had to be Peck, went through a lot to put this list together. It wasn't just a spur of the moment thing he had slammed together last night. The prick planned this and backed me into a corner with his "put your money where your mouth is" challenge. Well screw you, Peck. I'm not going to fall for it.

When he signed onto Facebook he found that Peck had posted all about it and at least a dozen people had already responded saying they loved the idea. His Twitter feed was also overflowing. If he blew it off now, he was never going to live it down. He had to find a way out of this without looking like a complete idiot. They'd laugh him out of school if he backed out. He couldn't let that be his legacy.

Pierce found a ray of hope when he saw the cost of everything. Just the standard equipment was going to run over ten thousand dollars. Then you had to add on the cost of the optional items. Peck would never be able to come up with the money.

He had just finished looking over the list when Cusack came into the room with his usual lack of grace. He tossed his books on his bed from six feet away. Two of them actually stayed where they landed, the third bounced off and hit the floor. Cusack was so intent on his iPhone that he didn't even notice Pierce was sitting at his desk. When he finally glanced up and saw him sitting there, Cusack stopped laughing and put the phone away so quickly that Pierce had a good idea what he had been looking at.

"So, what's so funny?"

Cusack squirmed for a few seconds before answering. "Some of the tweets about your wilderness challenge," he answered, obviously embarrassed. Then he added, "You really going to do it?"

"I doubt it. Peck will never get up enough money to finance the trip."

"Man, don't bet on it. It's all over campus. Peck and his friends are asking everyone to share it on Facebook, Twitter and everywhere else. This thing is hot. There are almost twelve thousand students here at UMaine. Peck says if he can get every student to donate just one dollar he can do it."

Pierce was stunned. He'd never thought of that. Peck had

really thought this thing out. Pierce doubted *every* student would donate a buck, but a lot of them would ... and some of them might even kick in more than that. This could really happen.

Later, when he went downstairs for dinner, most of the guys in the frat were there. Peck was sitting with his pal, Derick Stanley. When Pierce walked in, every head turned to look at him. He felt like a specimen under a microscope.

"So, Survivor Boy, you still up for the challenge?" Peck asked. There was a mocking tone to his voice that was impossible to miss and Pierce knew the Survivor Boy was a slur based on the *Survivorman* reality show, another of Pierce's favorites, in which Les Strand survives completely on his own for a week in hostile environments without the benefit of a camera crew. Every head in the room turned to hear his reply.

Fine, he thought. *If you want to play this game, I can play too.*

"Of course, you want to make a bet on it?"

"What kind of bet?" Peck asked.

"I'm not willing to try to beat the current record. I don't have the time for that. I need to get a job after I graduate, but I'll go for a month. If I make it, you get to try it too."

"No way," Peck replied. "I never said I was into that shit. You did. And if you're not willing to go the whole route, what's the sense of it?"

"A month is a month, man. A lot of the people on that show don't even make it that far. Some don't make it past the first few days. A month's enough to show I can do it. If it's not enough for you, that's fine. As it is, a month will blow most of my summer anyway."

"Fine, a month then," Peck agreed, but Pierce could see he wasn't happy about it.

"And," Pierce added, "I get to keep all the gear when I'm done."

He was pleased to see a look of disappointment on Peck's face. Obviously, the guy had thought about selling the gear and pocketing the cash.

"Fine," Peck finally answered. "But only if you make the whole month. If not, I get to keep it."

Pleased by Peck's reaction, Pierce decided to play the money card. "By the way, Peck, where do you intend to get the money for all the equipment I'll need? You going to spring for it yourself?"

"Not me," Peck answered. "But don't worry, I've already got over fifteen hundred of it."

"No way. Where'd you get that kind of money?" Pierce demanded.

"I set up a GoFundMe account. The donations are coming in like crazy. I guess a lot of people want to see you do this."

"Bullshit," Pierce told him.

"No bullshit, check it out," Peck said, and held up his phone.

Pierce stared at the screen. It showed that $1,654.02 had already been donated to the account. "That's my two cents by the way," Peck said before taking the phone back.

"Shit," Pierce swore under his breath, and headed for his room to check it out for himself.

The link to the GoFundMe account was the first thing he found when he signed onto his Facebook account. There was a picture of him watching *Alone* in which he was staring intently at the screen. The words "I could so do this" had been added along the bottom of the picture.

He started to click on the link, but paused to read some of the comments that had been posted. Hell, he didn't know half these people and every guy in the frat had shared it on his page already.

Sounds like a great idea. Good for him.

He won't make it a week!

A girl he didn't know had posted: *I'll double my donation if he does it naked.* ☺

There were dozens more, but he got the idea. Peck might actually be able to pull this off.

When he clicked onto the GoFundMe link, he got his first look at what Peck had posted.

My good friend Pierce Chambers will be graduating at the end of this semester and I'd like to give him a graduation present he'll never forget. Pierce loves Alone, *the survival show on the History*

Channel. Pierce would love to be on the show, but it takes a strong survivalist background he doesn't have, so his chances are slim to none of being selected. But we can make his dream come true, I'm starting this GoFundMe campaign to raise enough money to allow him to have his own, once in a lifetime, adventure this summer. The money raised will go toward purchasing the equipment supplied to all contestants on the show. It's quite a list … you can check it out for yourself on the History channel's web site. Pierce will tape his experience just like the contestants on the show. He'll try to live for 31 days on his own in the wild. One dollar, just one dollar from each UMaine student is all we need. That's less than you'd spend on a cup of coffee at Dunkin Donuts or Starbucks.

Pierce will post his recordings on YouTube when he completes the adventure. So, what do you say? Let's show the world that the University of Maine stands behind its students.

Good friend my ass, Pierce thought, but he had to admit Peck had created one hell of a campaign. He'd even be willing to contribute to it if it had been for someone else. Before he could log off the site another five-dollar donation popped up on the screen. That brought the one day total to close to two thousand dollars.

TWO

"Mike, look at this," Derick Stanley exclaimed and held his iPad up for Peck to see. "The total is up to $3,526.02 and it's only the second day!"

"Yeah, but we've still got a way to go. I'm not going to get too excited about it until we get a lot closer."

Despite what he said, Peck was thrilled at the way the money was coming in. They just had to keep the pressure on, keep the campaign alive. GoFundMe campaigns had a way of petering out after a few days.

"The thing we need to do now is get everybody talking about it. I've made up a bunch of flyers. We can pass them out, post them at the student union and put up them on all the notice boards on campus."

"Great idea," Pete Priolo said. "I'm going over to the union now. Give me a stack and I'll drop them off."

The flyers were a repeat of the GoFundMe post with the picture of Pierce sitting in front of the television watching *Alone*. A large heading, "Help Pierce Chambers, UMaine's own Survivor Man, Achieve His Dream," had been added above the picture. A link to the GoFundMe account was printed in red at the bottom. By the end of the day, the flyers would be all over campus.

"You really think Chambers will do it if you raise the money?" Derick Stanley asked.

"He'll have to," Peck answered. "He'll never live it down if he doesn't. Imagine how that would look on a résumé—'I backed out on a bet I agreed to because I never thought I'd have to live up to the challenge.'"

"Man, he'd never put that on a résumé."

"No, but employers are getting smart about social media. All they have to do is run a Google search and there it would be. No, he'll do it. We just need to raise the money."

"What if he does it? What if he makes it the whole time and comes out looking like a hero?"

"Don't worry, he won't," Peck assured him.

"Yeah, but what if he does?"

"He won't. We'll make sure of that. You don't think I'd actually let him succeed, do you?"

"But how … oh, I get it. You've got something planned, don't you?"

Peck didn't answer, but he didn't have to. The smile on his face said it all.

Pierce followed the GoFundMe account as closely as Peck and his cohorts did. But, while they cheered every time the total went up, Pierce cringed. After a week it had reached $8,524.02. The rate at which it was increasing had slowed, but it was still climbing every day. Pierce feigned nonchalance, but every time he crossed paths with Peck, the asshole would make it a point to inform him of how much the campaign had raised. He had even posted a sign outside the frat house, a big red thermometer, that he updated every day showing the total that had been donated.

At the end of the second week, the total had climbed to just over $10,000, and there were still three weeks left until graduation. After that there was little chance Peck would be able to reach the $15,000 goal he had set. Even if Peck didn't raise enough to send Pierce on his adventure into the wilderness, he had ruined his love of the show. He couldn't stand to watch it anymore while listening to the taunts and jeers from the guys in the frat.

With one week left, the total stood at $14,203.02. It stayed there for two days and then a flurry of last minute donations brought it to $14,452.02. Then it stalled.

Two days before graduation it still hadn't gone up. When Pierce came down for dinner, Peck was staring at this iPad. Pierce walked over, glanced at the screen and smiled. "Looks like you're not going to make it Peck. Too bad, all you needed was another $547.98. And I was *really* looking forward to it."

"I'm glad to hear that Chambers, because you are going," Peck told him as he typed in $547.98 and hit the Donate button. A second later the total updated to exactly $15,000. Pierce's heart sank.

Pierce looked around the room. Every frat brother was staring at him to see his response. Now he had to decide whether to live up to the challenge or back down. Neither choice thrilled him, but it only took a minute to realize he didn't *have* a choice. "Good, because *I so wanted to do this*," he told Peck.

Peck's smile faltered for the briefest second, and then it was back. Pierce had the distinct feeling that there was something he should know, but didn't. Suddenly, he had lost his appetite, but he sat and ate so Peck wouldn't know how anxious he was about his upcoming *adventure*.

Once he was back in his room, Pierce logged onto the History channel website, clicked on SHOWS, and then ALONE. Once there, he went to the Menu and selected Bios and Packing Lists to see which ten additional items each contestant had taken with them on their challenge. Then he realized he had no idea where he was going. He needed to know that before he could decide on what to bring. In the first two seasons, all the contestants had been taken to Vancouver Island. Season Three had taken place in Patagonia. Neither of those was possible for him. For one thing, Vancouver was all the way out on the West coast and Patagonia was in South America. Both of those were outside the United States. He didn't have a passport. So … in the U.S and on the East coast. It was going to have to be somewhere here in Maine. That made the most sense. But would it be on the coast, or inland? Salt or fresh water? That would make a difference in the gear he chose. A quick search on Google Earth confirmed what he thought. If he was going to be truly alone, it would have to be on a lake somewhere. The coast was just too well-traveled by tourists and fishing boats. He wasn't even sure Peck was going to able to find a place isolated enough inland. With that bit of knowledge, he went back to the lists to make his selections.

Pierce went looking for Peck the next morning to work out

the details of the challenge. He had been thinking about it ever since the donations started to mount up and had some conditions he was going to insist on.

Peck was sitting in the dining room with Stanley, his constant companion. They both grinned at Pierce when he walked in, but their grins disappeared when Pierce walked over and sat down with them.

"You here to back out?" Peck asked, loud enough for everyone in the room to hear.

"No, I'm here to work out the details. I've got conditions."

Peck frowned at him and then grinned before answering. "What kind of conditions?"

"First, I want to know where I'll be doing this. It has to be in the U.S. because I don't have a passport."

"No problem," Peck responded. "I'm sure we can find a nice spot right here in Maine."

Pierce slid a printed list across the table. "Good. Here are the rest."

Peck just stared at the list without picking it up. Pierce read aloud from his copy so that everyone in the dining hall could hear the conditions he wanted placed on the challenge.

A fresh water source must be available at the site

Emergency medical aid must be available within 30 minutes of a call for assistance

Scheduled pickup to be no later than noon on Day 31

The two allotted fleece/wool shirts will be replaced by two long-sleeved flannel shirts (Reason – weather in Maine in summer)

The following ten items selected from the optional items from the *Alone* website will be provided:

1 saw
1 axe
1 multi-seasonal sleeping bag that fits within provided backpack
1 2-quart cast iron pot, includes lid
1 ferro rod set
1 300-yard roll of nylon single filament fishing line (10# test)
25 assorted hooks (no lures)
1 primitive bow (60 pound pull) with 6 arrows (must be predominately made of wood)
5 lbs of beef jerky (protein)
2 lbs of rice and 1 lb of salt
1 hunting knife

After he was done, all eyes turned to Peck. "Fine," Peck told him.

"Here's the list of equipment you slipped under my door. I've indicated the things I'll pick up myself. I don't want you buying me boots that are two sizes too small. I'll send you a total cost and you can send the money to my PayPal account. You can get the rest of it."

"Fine," Peck agreed again.

"Good, we can start on July first. That will give you time to get the gear together and find a spot. We'll meet back here then."

Without another word, Pierce went to his room to finish packing. He wanted to head for home and Katie as soon as graduation was over.

THREE

The enormity of what he was doing set in as he watched his classmates march to the podium to receive their diplomas. *It's actually happening.* It wasn't the challenge he was thinking about, but what was occurring in his life. One phase of it was ending and another beginning. He wouldn't be coming back here next year. He'd either be working, or looking for a job. He had years of work ahead of him. In the face of that, thirty-one days of solitude in the Maine woods would be a walk in the park. He'd really enjoyed camping as a kid. Before he had gone off to college he had spent most of his summers in the woods. By the time they called his name to come up for his diploma, he was actually getting excited about his coming adventure ... and he had Peck, of all people, to thank for it.

On the ride back home, Pierce thought about what he was going to do to get ready for his thirty-one days in the wild. Ordering and watching every episode of *Alone* was on top of his list. After that he planned to study every survival book he could lay his hands on. A guide to edible plants native to Maine was also something he needed. He wouldn't be able to take it with him, but he could study it. Pierce didn't know how many edible plants there were in Maine, but there could be hundreds he could eat if he could find and identify them. Katie was okay with it. She had been following everything on Facebook and Twitter and she wanted him to do it just to spite Peck. His biggest problem was going to be how to tell his parents what he was planning. His mom would be worried, and his dad would probably be all over his ass about finding a job.

Pierce didn't bring up the subject of the trip to his parents until two days after he was home. They were eating dinner when his dad asked him what his plans were for finding a job and, eventually, a place of his own.

"I'm hoping to find a teaching position. I've already sent out a bunch of résumés. If I do get a teaching job, I won't have to start until school starts in the fall."

"What are you going to do until then?" his mother asked.

Pierce took a minute before answering. "I'm going to spend thirty-one days by myself in the woods up north."

"Why on earth would you want to do that?" his mother asked.

"This is going to sound weird," Pierce answered. Then he then told them about the challenge.

His mother was completely against it, and had no problem telling him so. "Alone? With no shelter and nothing to eat? That's ridiculous. I forbid it."

"Not so fast," his father told her. "I think it's a good idea."

Pierce and his mother were both shocked by his response.

"If Pierce can do this, it will be good for him. It'll show him he can depend on himself. And, if he can't do it, he'll learn a lot about himself. I wish I would have had a chance to do something like that when I was his age."

"You can't be serious?" his mother answered.

"Of course I'm serious. Good for you, Pierce."

"What about Katie? What does she think?" his mother asked, playing the girlfriend trick.

"Oh, she's all for it. She's going to help me practice for it."

Nothing was said for the rest of the meal.

The next morning his dad offered to help him with his plans. "Let's take a trip to Barnes & Noble. I'll buy you a couple of field guides you're going to need."

"I can't take them with me, you know."

"No, but you've got over a month to study them."

Pierce had to admit it was a good idea—he didn't bother to tell his dad that he had already thought of it.

"So tell me about this thing you've got going on and why you decided to do it," his dad asked on the way to the mall.

So Pierce did. He told him about watching *Alone* and the

other survival shows, and Peck's dare, and how it got out of hand on social media. "In the end I really had no choice. It was either agree to do it, or come off as a complete braggart and a phony."

"And that's why you're doing this?"

"It was in the beginning, but now I'm actually excited about it. I want to prove to myself I can do it."

"Okay, so what can I do to help you?"

"Nothing, I'm supposed to do this on my own."

"You need to *stay in the woods on your own*, you don't have to prepare on your own."

"Maybe, but Katie's already volunteered to help. But let me think about it." Pierce told him as they arrived at the mall.

"Dad, just park," Pierce told his father after they had driven up and down three rows of cars looking for an open parking spot.

"Where? The lot's full?"

"No it's not," Pierce answered. "There are plenty of spots out on the end. We don't have to park right up in the front, you know."

"One more try," his father insisted. "If I don't find one on the next pass I'll park out in no-man's-land."

"There's one," his dad announced as he saw a red minivan backing out of a spot at the end of the row they had just entered. The van backed out and turned so it was facing them. Before they could get around it, a blue compact zipped into the space it had just vacated.

"Shit," Pierce's father swore.

"Dad … just park. It's not that far a walk."

With a sigh of defeat, his dad pulled into an open space all the way at the end of the aisle.

The walk to the store was still no more than a hundred yards. On the way, two cars backed out of their parking spaces. Pierce smiled, but didn't say anything as they walked past the empty spots. One was right on the end of the row, the other was two spaces in. "Murphy's Law," his father commented and shook his head.

Inside the Barnes & Noble store, Pierce had no idea where to look for field guides on edible plants in the Northeast. After five minutes of aimlessly wandering the aisles, he broke down and asked a girl who had just returned to the help desk. She directed him to the section he needed.

After some serious consideration, he selected a copy of Leda Meredith's *Northeast Foraging* from the shelf. Looking at the cover it appeared to be just what he was looking for—*"120 wild and flavorful edibles from beach plums to wineberries."* More important was the blurb at the bottom of the cover—*"A book that wild food gatherers of all skill levels will want to own."* He really liked the *"all skill levels"* part. When he opened it, he was pleased to find it was categorized by seasons. He would be there for the month of July, so he would only have to study the edible plants that would be available then.

He was going to settle for that when his dad pulled one from the shelf and handed it to him. It was the *National Audubon Society Field Guide to Mushrooms*.

"I don't know if I want to mess around with mushrooms," Pierce told him, and started to put the book back.

"Are you sure? his dad asked.

Pierce considered it. "What the hell. It can't hurt, right?"

His dad laughed. "As long as you only eat the good ones. And don't tell your mother I said that. As a matter of fact, don't even mention mushrooms to her."

"Good idea," Pierce agreed.

Pierce picked Katie up the next morning to go shopping for the gear he needed. She was waiting outside when he arrived. "So, where are we going?" she asked when she opened the door and climbed inside.

"Freeport. L.L.Bean should have everything I need."

"Freeport's forty minutes. Why don't you just order it online?"

"Because I need to make sure it all fits. I refuse to order boots online."

"So let's see the list of things you need to get," she said on the drive over.

Pierce reached into his pocket, pulled out a folded sheet of paper and handed it to her. "I'm getting all the stuff marked with an asterisk. Peck is getting the rest of it."

Katie studied it for several minutes before speaking. The items Pierce had opted to buy were:

1 pair of high leg hunting boots
2 pairs of Outdoor Pants (can unzip into shorts)
1 t-shirt
2 fleece or wool shirts (hooded or unhooded)
3 pairs of wool socks
1 hat (brimmed, wool or baseball)
1 bandana or shemagh
1 pair gloves
1 light outdoor jacket
2 pairs of underwear
1 rain jacket and rain trousers
1 thermal underwear (long)
1 pair of gaiters
1 pair of Crocs, Teva sandals or Keen sandals
1 backpack
1 flint or ferro rod set
1 saw
1 axe
1 primitive bow (60 pound pull)
6 arrows (must be predominately made of wood)

"You're not going to need some of this stuff. Can you substitute if you want to?"

"Like what?" Pierce asked.

"Well, it's July. You don't need any fleece or wool shirts. Something lightweight would be better. Then there's the high leg hunting boots. A pair of lightweight hiking shoes would make more sense."

When they got to L.L.Bean the parking lot was only half full, but that was only because it was a weekday in early June. Once school was out and the flatlanders started to arrive, it would be nearly impossible to find a spot.

"Let's start with boots," Pierce suggested once they were in the store.

The selection was overwhelming, but he took Katie's advice and looked for a pair of lightweight hiking shoes instead of the high leg hunting boots on his list. In the end he settled on a pair of waterproof Gore-Tex hiking boots for $199.00.

"What's next on the list?" he asked after putting the boots in a shopping cart.

"Pants, ones that can unzip into shorts."

"Unzip into shorts? I've never seen anything like that."

They found them with a little help from a salesperson, and two pairs of Timberledge Zip-off pants went into the cart along with the hiking boots.

Katie consulted the list and saw that the next item was a t-shirt. "I have plenty of those at home, what's next?" Pierce told her.

"Two fleece or wool shirts (hooded or unhooded), but I think you should go for something a bit lighter. You won't need wool shirts in July."

"Good idea. Let's find something a bit more seasonal."

After browsing through the shirts, Pierce settled on two long-sleeved Tropic Wear shirts. They were lightweight and breathable with a UPF rating of 50+. The material would also wick moisture away on hot days.

"Why not short sleeves?" Katie asked. "Don't you think they'd be more comfortable?"

"I can always roll the sleeves up and I can keep them down at night if the mosquitoes are bad. I could even cut the sleeves off if I wanted."

"Right," she agreed.

Next, three pairs of wool socks, a bandana, a pair of gloves and a light outdoor jacket went in the cart.

"What about the underwear?" Katie asked.

"I have those at home."

"No fun. I want to help you pick them out," she said, and laughed when his face turned red.

Katie read the next three items off the list—a rain jacket and trousers, a set of thermal underwear and a pair of gaiters. "What are gaiters?" she asked him.

"Damned if I know. Let's ask."

Gaiters turned out to be like the lower half of a pair of pants that could be strapped around the leg under the knee and then under your boots. They were waterproof and designed to keep snow out of your pants.

"I don't think I'll be needing those in July," Pierce told her.

"Don't be stupid, take them and the thermal underwear. You never know what you might need. Just being waterproof might be important."

The gaiters went into the growing pile of equipment in his cart. Next up—a pair of Crocs, Teva sandals or Keen sandals. Pierce opted for the Keen Newport sandals because they had a closed toe and were made of leather. "I can't see myself walking around the woods in an open-toe pair of sandals. I'd wind up with a stick in my foot. No thank you. And, if I needed to, I could cannibalize them for the leather. Now let's find a backpack."

There were several backpacks available. After trying them on, Pierce chose the White Mountain model. It had a steel frame and a capacity of 4.638 cubic inches and weighed just under six pounds. Now all he needed, other than the bow and arrows, was a saw, an axe and a ferro rod fire starter. The saw and axe were no problem, but L.L.Bean didn't have a ferro rod in stock. He'd have to order that from the internet.

"Why not just use the one you have at home?" Katie asked as they stood in front of a selection of bows.

"Mine's a compound bow. I need a primitive, mostly wooden bow. They don't have one, so I'm guess I'm going to have to look online for that."

"Wait. I almost missed something. You need one, 300-yard roll of nylon single filament fishing line and 25 assorted hooks."

"Right. That would be a bad thing to forget. I guess I'd better get a fishing license while I'm at it."

"When's the last time you actually went camping?" Katie asked.

"Back in high school. A bunch of us went down to the White Mountains. We hiked in and slept in one of the lean-tos they have along some of the trails."

"I hope you're going to practice before you head out on this adventure of yours."

When he didn't answer, Katie shook her head and said, "You haven't thought of that yet, have you?"

"Not exactly," he answered.

"So let me get this right. You're getting a strange bow you've never shot before, but you're going to rely on it in the woods. You've probably never started a fire with one of those ferro things either, have you?"

"No," he admitted.

"Well, you're going to need to go camping and practice some of this stuff. Do you have a tent and sleeping bag?"

"Uh, no."

"Then you'd better buy them. You need to practice."

"I guess you're right. Let's go look at tents."

"Here's one I like," she said, standing in front of an Adventure Dome 2-person tent.

Pierce got down on his hands and knees, crawled into it and lay down. Katie crawled in after him and lay down next to him. "Nice," he said when he crawled out, "but it's $169 bucks. Peck isn't going to pay for this. I have to. I'll get a cheap tarp and use it. That's what I'm going to have to do when I'm out there."

"Yeah, well I'm not sleeping under a tarp. Get the tent."

"You? What do you mean, you're not sleeping under a tarp?"

"Just what I said. Me. I'm going to go with you. Now let's go find some sleeping bags."

"You sure?" he asked.

"Hell, yes. You're going to be gone the entire month of July. I want to spend as much time with you as I can before that."

It was Katie who picked out the sleeping bags, two flannel-lined bags rated at forty degrees. They were $69.99 each on sale. "I'll pay for mine," Katie said as she put them in the cart.

Peck was making different plans for Chambers' trip to the woods of northern Maine. He ordered everything he needed to get for Pierce, plus the "special" items he and Derick Stanley would need, online. He was bringing Stanley along as a safety net. He had no intention of being alone in the woods if something went wrong.

The first thing on his list of special items was a pair of

portable speakers he could connect to his iPhone. Then he assembled a collection of recordings that included grunting bears, moose, bobcats, coyotes, owls, loons and even a wolf. His favorite was a deep, throaty, growling dog that gave him the shivers even though he knew it was just a recording. Pierce might, or might not, encounter the actual animals on the tape, but he wouldn't know that. Peck even recorded some grunts and guttural growls that no animal had ever made. These would be the icing on the cake.

Next he ordered bear, moose and bobcat hair from an out-doors website. He planned to leave these attached to branches for Pierce to find after he heard the "noises" in the night.

Well, "I can so do that" boy, we'll see how you handle things that go bump in the night. I'm betting you won't last a week after the fun starts.

His biggest problem would be finding a location. It had to be remote enough to ensure Chambers would be isolated from civilization, but was still accessible enough to allow him to get Chambers and all his gear to it. Google Earth was a good start-ing point, but that's all it was, a start. He actually had to get out into the North Country and scout around.

It took him two weeks, but he finally found what he thought would be an acceptable spot. It was a small lake twenty miles from the Canadian border. It looked like it could be reached on an ATV via an old logging road. It wasn't perfect, but it might do. He'd have to make a trip up there to see if it was what he was looking for. After taking a screenshot of the area he was ready to scope it out. He'd call Stanley to ask if he wanted to go with him since he was going to be up there too.

"Derick, I think I found a spot for Chambers. It's up north. You want to take a ride up there with me to check it out?"

"Sure, when do you want to do it?"

"Tomorrow. Meet me at the frat house."

"What time?"

"Eight. It's a long ride."

Stanley was waiting at the frat house when Peck arrived driving a pickup and towing a trailer with an ATV loaded on the back.

"What's that for?" Stanley asked pointing to the ATV when he climbed into the passenger seat.

"So we can check out the area once we get there."

"So, how far is it?" Stanley asked when they were on the road.

"At least six hours, probably more since I'm hauling a trailer."

"Good, that means we have time to stop for breakfast, right?"

Peck glanced over and glared at him. "Breakfast? Didn't you eat before we met?"

"No. Just coffee on the way over. I thought we'd stop and get something on the way."

"Well, I hope you like Egg McMuffins, because we don't have time to be screwing around with breakfast."

"Why not? We'll be there by one or two o'clock."

"To get there, yeah. Then we'll probably be there a few hours and then we have another six-hour ride home. As it is, we'll be getting back after midnight."

"Well, stop soon because I'm hungry," Stanley mumbled, obviously disappointed.

They went through the drive through just off campus. Stanley got two Egg McMuffin meals, a coffee and an orange juice. Peck just got a coffee. After finishing the second McMuffin, Stanley asked where they were going.

"A little town near the Canadian border named Tinkers Falls. I found it on Google Earth."

"What's there?"

"I have no idea. I'm interested in the lake a couple of miles from town."

"You got a map," Stanley asked.

"Who needs a map? I've got a GPS and the coordinates."

They came across the first Visit the Bigfoot Museum sign fifty miles from Tinkers Falls.

"Hey, we should check it out," Stanley said as they drove past.

Peck shook his head. "We won't have time for shit like that. We need to check the woods out."

They saw the next sign ten miles later. This one said, See a life-sized Bigfoot at the Bigfoot Museum, along with a picture of a child standing next to a huge Bigfoot replica.

"You know, maybe we *should* stop there," Peck said after seeing the picture.

They found the museum on the main street in Tinkers Falls. "There it is," Stanley announced when they were almost past it. For all the signs they had been seeing for the last fifty miles, the "Bigfoot Museum" name on the front of the building was so small it was easy to miss. Luckily, there weren't many cars parked on the street and Peck was able to park the pickup and trailer within half a block of the place.

When they got out and walked back, the front door was locked and the lights were out inside. A sign on the door, however, proclaimed, Ring Bell for Service. Peck did, and a minute later a woman opened the door to admit him. After they each paid the ten dollar admission fee, Peck and Stanley found that the entire museum consisted only of two large rooms, but they were stuffed with Bigfoot memorabilia. There were several fuzzy pictures, supposedly of Bigfoots in the woods, but the most impressive was the full-sized replica in the second room. It stood at least seven feet tall. The name plaque in front of it declared it was a Pomoola. *Hah, even Chambers would feel like a dwarf next to this thing.*

"Would you like a picture standing next to him?" the woman who ran the museum asked.

Peck was about to tell her no, but then smiled and answered, "Sure, why not, but what's with the Pomoola name tag?"

"That's what we call them up here. It's an old Indian name."

"Oh, okay," Peck answered, and handed the woman his phone. After she had snapped the shot, Peck took several more from different angles, most of them close-ups. By the time they got out of the museum it was too late to scout the woods where Peck wanted to take Chambers. Now he had a decision to make: go home and come back another day, or stay the night. After talking it over with Stanley they decided to stay, but only after Peck agreed to pay for the room out of the GoFundMe account.

The only place to stay in town turned out to be the Tinkers Falls Motel, right next to the museum. Stanley waited in the truck while Peck went into the office to get a room.

Just like at the museum, Peck had to ring a bell on the counter to let someone know he was there. An old man with white hair and a day's worth of stubble on his face answered the bell's ring.

He looked at Peck and then outside at Stanley sitting in the truck. "Yes, sir. Can I help you?" he asked.

"Yes, I'd like to get a room."

The old fellow glanced from Peck to Stanley and frowned before asking, "One room or two?"

"One."

The old man shifted his gaze to Stanley and asked, "Two full-sized beds or one queen?"

Peck almost choked before answering. "Two full-sized beds, of course."

"Of course," the man replied with a slight smile on his face that reminded Peck of Chambers' smirk.

Peck was tempted to say "fuck it" and leave, but he didn't want to drive an hour back to the last motel he had passed on the drive up. Instead he gave the man his credit card, signed the receipt and got the key to the room.

When he got back in the pickup, he slammed the door and mumbled "Fuck you, old man," under his breath.

"What's the matter?" Stanley asked.

"Son of a bitch wanted to know if I wanted two full-sized beds or a queen. Do I look like a queer to you?"

"Fuck no," Stanley told him.

In the morning they headed out to scout the area Peck had found on Google Earth. "Keep an eye out for an old logging road," he told Stanley as they got close to the coordinates he had entered into his GPS. A few minutes later they saw it. The entrance was blocked off by a locked metal fence with a large No Trespassing sign. The road was overgrown with weeds and looked like it hadn't been used in years.

"Now what?" Stanley asked when he saw the sign.

"Now we check it out," Peck answered, and drove another mile down the road before stopping and unloading the ATV.

Peck had to ignore the No Trespassing sign and drive

around a locked gate across the entrance to a logging road, but that didn't bother him. He was thrilled to see the old road had deteriorated to not much more than an overgrown trail.

Stanley sat next to Peck on the ATV. "Hang on, because we're going to be going over some rough ground on the way to the lake," Peck told him.

Stanley dismissed the warning. "Don't worry about me, I'll be fine,"

Will you? Peck thought and gave the ATV's throttle a quick twist. Stanley, who hadn't expected it, was thrown back in his seat hard enough to jolt him.

"Hey, take it easy."

"I told you to hang on," Peck told him, silently laughing to himself.

They had to clear it of brush and small trees in several places as he and Stanley made their way to the lake. *This is good. It means no one has been out here in a long time.*

"Stop," Stanley exclaimed and grabbed Peck's arm. "Did you see that?"

"See what?"

"I'm not sure. I think it was a bear, but it was standing up on its hind legs."

"I didn't see it. I was watching the trail. But, if it was a bear, it's long gone by now. The ATV would have scared it away."

"I don't know. It looked pretty big for a bear."

"Good. It'll keep Pierce company while he's out here."

"What about us, we're going to be out here too."

"Don't worry. I'll bring something for that."

The old road ended at the end of a marsh filled with cattails and weeds. "This is perfect," Peck told Stanley. "This place has got to be full of mosquitoes and snakes and shit."

Stanley slapped at something on his neck. When he pulled his hand away there was a smear of blood and a dead mosquito. "No shit. Let's get out of here."

"Now we have to find a place to set up our camp," Peck answered, and backed the ATV up until he found a spot wide enough to turn around.

When they reached a side trail Peck had seen on his way

in. It was even more overgrown than the one he was on. After a moment's indecision, he decided to give it a try. It led to a stand of pine trees out of sight of the road. "This is ideal" he told Stanley. "It's far enough from Chambers that we can easily get to him, but he wouldn't be able to get to us. Not if he plays by the rules, anyway. If he does find us, we can say we're were there for his safety."

As he turned the ATV around to head back to his pickup he never noticed that he was being watched by several pairs of curious, brown eyes.

FOUR

"What's that for?" Katie asked when Pierce unloaded a propane camp stove from the trunk of his car.

"It's for cooking. What do you think?"

"Oh no, you don't. You're not going to have one of those when you're up north, so you're not going to use it now. You're here to practice for your trip."

Pierce looked longingly at the stove and then put it back in the trunk. "I guess you're right. If I'm going to do this I might as well start now. We can gather some firewood after we get the tent set up. Or would you rather just sleep under a tarp like I'm going to have to do when I'm gone?"

"There's an idea. You can sleep under a tarp and I'll take the tent," she answered.

Pierce wasn't sure if she was serious or not until she grinned and laughed at him. "I wish I had my phone out right now so I could take a picture of your face. And don't worry, we'll share the tent. Besides, you don't even have a tarp."

"No," Pierce admitted. "And it's a good thing, because I think we're going to get some rain."

Putting up the tent should have been easy, and it would have been if he had practiced it at home. It only had three fiberglass poles and six stakes, but the poles had to be put in just right. They were still fumbling with it when the first peal of thunder rumbled out of the west. Katie started counting. Eight seconds later they heard the sound of thunder.

"We can always sleep in the car if we have to," he told her as they scrambled to finish setting the tent up.

"No way, let's just get this done," she answered. They

finished just as the first drops of rain reached them.

"Hah, success," Katie laughed and ducked through the door.

"What about the stakes?" Pierce called after her.

"Forget them, we can do that later."

"No. I'll get them," he called to her. He just managed to pound them in before the rain got heavy and he followed her into the tent. Once there, he turned and zipped the opening closed. Inside, it was dry, but the rain beat a steady drum on the top and sides of the tent.

"It's a good thing this thing's waterproof and has a floor," Katie said. "Too bad you won't have one of these on your trip."

"No kidding," he answered. The tent definitely had its advantages, but once inside, with the rain beating down on them, it seemed a lot smaller that it had when they had climbed inside the one back at L.L.Bean's. And it was only going to get smaller when they brought in the air mattress, sleeping bags and some gear. Neither of them could stand up in it. The tent's height only reached fifty-four inches. Their only options were to sit, crouch or crawl. It was seven and a half feet long and five feet wide, plenty of room for sleeping and storing some gear. He wasn't claustrophobic, but he could see it closing in on him if he had to spend all day in it.

Pierce opened the tent door enough to peek out at the campsite. The car was parked fifty feet away, barely visible through the downpour. "What about our stuff," he asked. "We're going to need it tonight."

"Wait until the rain lets up a bit. Then you can make a dash for it," she told him.

"Me? What happened to we?"

"*We* left when the rain started. I'll wait in here and you can toss the stuff in to me. I'll stack it. Just get the sleeping bags and the air mattress. Oh, and the wine. Make sure you get the wine. We can get the other things later."

They sat and listened to the rain, making small talk until it tapered off a bit twenty minutes later. The sky still lit up with distant flashes of lightning, and thunder still rolled in the distance, but the downpour had slackened. "Go now, before it gets heavy again," Katie said, and pushed him toward the door.

Pierce ran for the car, being careful not to slip on the wet ground. He didn't need to slip and land in one of the puddles the rain had created. When he got to the car he opened the trunk, grabbed the sleeping bags, slammed the lid closed and ran back to the tent.

"Get the air mattress and the wine," Katie called out as she moved the sleeping bags to the back of the tent.

Pierce did as he was told and sprinted back to the car. When he got there he opened the door and climbed into the passenger seat. He needed a breather. Besides, the wine was in a bag in the back seat along with the crackers and cheese. He was about to get out and go back around to the trunk when the rain started to come down heavy again. *Screw this*, he thought and started the car and turned the heater on to warm up and dry off a bit.

A minute later his cell phone rang. "What are you doing out there?" Katie asked when he answered.

"Just warming up and trying to dry off a bit. I'll be back as soon as it lets up."

"Okay, but don't be too long."

Fifteen minutes later he was still sitting in the car enjoying the heater when his phone rang again. "The hell with this. Grab the wine and air mattress and get back here."

Pierce looked at the tent. In the pouring rain, the fifty feet separating it from the car looked more like a hundred. Rivulets of rain water ran like small rivers and puddles had formed in low spots across the void separating them. Sighing, he turned off the ignition, grabbed the bag with the wine, cheese and crackers, popped the trunk for the air mattress and made a dash for it. By the time he got there he was pretty much soaked.

Katie had the door open and he passed the bag and mattress through. "Wait, shoes off before you get in," she told him as he started to crawl through the door.

"Right," he agreed. A second later he was sitting with most of his body inside the tent and his feet sticking out the door where they were out of the rain because of the tent's built-in canopy, but just barely.

"Leave them out there," Katie said as he started to pick them up to bring them inside. "We don't need mud all over the floor," she admonished him when it looked like he might bring them in anyway. Instead, he tucked them as far under the canopy as he could and zipped the door closed behind him.

Inside, Katie had the sleeping bags unzipped and spread out, one over the other, to make a soft, warm cover over the floor. "This one's yours," she said patting the top one that he was dripping on.

It was dry and warm—well, at least warmer—inside the tent than it was outside. That didn't keep Pierce from shivering in his wet clothes. "Take those off and wrap up in your sleeping bag," Katie told him when she saw him shivering.

Pierce struggled out of his wet t-shirt and jeans. He threw them past her onto a bare spot on the tent's floor and then wrapped himself in his sleeping bag.

"Now let's have that wine," she said, when he had stripped and wrapped the sleeping bag around himself.

"Shit," he swore as soon as he saw it. "I left the corkscrew in the car."

"Well, I think you're going to have to go back and get it," Katie told him.

"No way. I'm not climbing back into those wet clothes and I'm not running out there in my underwear."

"Why not?" she laughed, "You look cute in your underwear."

"I don't care. I'm still not going back out there until it stops raining."

"Fine, where is it?" she asked.

"In the canvas bag in the trunk with the coffee and other stuff."

"Okay, I'll get it," she said and then stripped down to her panties, bra and tennis shoes. "What? I'm not getting my clothes soaked," she told him.

Then she was out of the tent and streaking toward the car. When she got there, she popped the trunk open, grabbed the canvas bag with the corkscrewand her backpack. She was on her way back in less than a minute.

As quick as she was, she was still soaked when she arrived at the tent. Like Pierce, she sat with her feet outside and slipped her tennis shoes off. Then she crawled all the way in. He stared at her. Her wet bra was practically see-through and her nipples stood out like gum drops just waiting to be nibbled.

"Down boy," she laughed and dug a pair shorts and a sports bra out of her backpack. Then she ducked under her sleeping bag to put them on. A minute later, her panties and bra joined his shirt and jeans on the tent floor.

"Ta-da," she said and laughed at the disappointed look on his face. Then she handed him the bottle of wine and rummaged in the bag for the corkscrew. She found it and passed it over before setting out the cheese and crackers. "It doesn't look like we'll be making a fire tonight, but at least we won't go hungry."

"If it stops raining we can use the grill and have hamburgers," he told her.

"Maybe … if it stops raining. Or maybe I'll just send you out for a pizza."

The wine was Ami Amore, a sweet red that Katie had picked out. The cheese was a sharp cheddar and the crackers were Town House. They didn't have any glasses in the tent so they had to drink from the bottle. The same was true for the cheese—no knife, so they just took bites off the block.

By the time they finished the wine, a steady rain was falling and it was starting to get dark. "We need the light," Katie told him, referring to the electric lantern they had brought with them.

"Yeah," Pierce agreed, "but who's going to get it?"

"Sounds like a job for my knight in shining armor. Just slip on your tennis shoes and run. Grab anything you can out of the trunk while you're there. You can wait in the car while I set up the air mattress. I'll call you when it's ready."

"Fine," he agreed, even though he wasn't all that anxious to go back outside.

Pierce felt the cold air on his naked skin as soon as he opened the tent door. "Damn, that's cold," he said as he slipped on this wet tennis shoes. As soon as they were on, he crabbed his way out of the tent and raced to the car where he sat and waited for Katie to call. It didn't take long, but it felt like an eternity. He was about to call her and ask her what was she was doing when his phone rang.

"Grab what you can and come back," she told him.

"Be there in a minute. Have the door open." Then he ended the call and raced to the back of the car.

Once he had the trunk open he grabbed the light, his bag of clothes and the small cooler that held soda, water, two apples and a foot-long, oven-roasted chicken sandwich from Subway. Before he slammed the trunk shut he grabbed the bottle of white wine that was chilling in the larger cooler with the rest of their food. Then he ran for the tent. When he got back he handed everything to Katie, slipped off his tennis shoes and crawled back inside. While he was gone Katie had inflated the air mattress and set it up at the far end of the tent. At sixty inches wide and seventy-eight inches long it almost covered the entire floor. She had zipped the sleeping bags together to make one bag they could both fit in. As soon as he was inside the tent, she tossed him a towel she must have had in her backpack.

When Pierce was dry, he rummaged in his bag of clothes and came out with a dry pair of jeans, underwear and a short-sleeved sweat shirt he had packed just in case the night got cold. Now he was glad he had it. Katie laughed while he struggled to get them on in the confined space of the tent.

When Pierce got the shirt over his head and looked at Katie she was holding the second bottle of wine. "What's this? You're not trying to get me drunk, are you?"

"Maybe."

"Right," she laughed and put it in the cooler. "We don't have to drink it. Let's see what we have. I'm still hungry." She took out the apples and water, set them aside and then unwrapped the sub.

"What's on it?" she asked lifting the top and peering inside.

"Oven-roasted chicken, lettuce, tomato, onions and mayo."

"Good choice … except for the onions, but I can pick those off. You want half, or is this all for me?

"Of course, I want half. Hand it over."

"Okay, but you should open the wine. Water just doesn't sound right with a sub."

By this time it was really getting dark and Katie turned the lantern on. It lit the interior of the tent with a stark, fluorescent, white light. "Well, it's not as romantic as candlelight, but it's probably a lot safer in a tent," she told him.

Pierce opened the wine and once again they had to drink it out of the bottle. By the time sandwich was gone, they had finished half of it.

"Maybe we should save the rest for tomorrow," she said when he handed it to her after taking a sip.

"We can't, the cork won't go back in. We either have to drink it or pour it out."

"Well, I can't see pouring out good wine," Katie said with a smile and took another sip from the bottle.

"Damn," Pierce swore after they had killed the bottle.

What's the matter?" Katie asked.

"I have to piss. I wonder if I can do it out the door?"

"Don't you dare. Do it outside.

"Shit," Pierce swore, and stripped down to bare skin. The he dashed out, ran a few feet from the tent and relieved himself. When he got back Katie was naked. He laughed and reached for her but she pushed him away.

"You're soaking wet and it's my turn. Now I have to pee."

"Be my guest," he said, and opened the tent flap for her.

"Thanks," she told him and crawled over to the tent's door. Then she took a deep breath and dashed outside. She didn't go far, only running around to the side of the tent where she peed in the grass. She was back inside in less than three minutes. Pierce had already dried off and was in the sleeping bag.

As soon as he was inside he tossed her the towel. "Dry off and climb in, then I'll turn out the light."

Once she was snuggled next to him he flicked the light off. The tent immediately went completely dark. With the overcast sky and rain, no light came in from outside. It was like being deep underground in a cave. "This is what I'm going to miss most when I'm in the woods," he said as he wrapped her in his arms.

"No, this is what you're going to miss most," she told him as she crawled on top of him.

Pierce woke to the weight of an arm on his side and a warm

body pressed up against his back. Diffused, early-morning sunlight filled the tent, illuminating the interior with a warm glow. He lay there for a minute savoring the feel of Katie's body against his. This is what he was going to miss the most. He tried not to think about waking up in the woods, alone. If she rolled over right now and asked him not to go, he'd probably say yes.

FIVE

Stanley kept an eye on the woods as Peck maneuvered the ATV over the old logging road. Several times he thought he saw movement in the trees. Most times it was just a quick glimpse in the shadows, but once he was sure he saw a bear staring back at him. He might have mentioned it to Peck, but he didn't want to get blown off again. Once was enough.

When they reached the locked fence at the end of the trail, he climbed off the ATV while Peck drove it around the fence. When he looked back at the way they had come, someone, or something, was silhouetted against the horizon. It was only there for a second, and then it was gone. Whatever it was—probably a bear like Peck said—gave him the chills. He wouldn't want to be out here in these woods by himself. He was starting to regret agreeing to camping out with Peck after they dropped Chambers off out here. He mentioned what he had seen on the ride back to the frat house where he had left his car.

"I thought I saw something following us while we were driving back from that lake. Then, when you were driving around that gate, I looked back and saw someone standing in the middle of the old road. He was only there for a second and then he was gone. It gave me the creeps."

"What do you mean *he*?"

Stanley hesitated before answering. "It looked like a man. A really big man."

"You said you only saw it for a second. Maybe it was a bear, or a moose. Those things are really big."

"I don't know, but I didn't think it was a bear, or a moose. I got the impression it was a man. A big man."

"Okay, so it was a man. If he was in the woods he was trespassing too. I don't think we have anything to worry about."

"Yeah … but what if it was … ah, you know, a Bigfoot?"

Peck gave him an incredulous look. "Oh, come on. A Bigfoot! Don't be ridiculous. That shit's just for the tourists and those dumb reality shows Chambers likes. If there were really Bigfoots anywhere, people would have found them already. That shit back at that museum, it's all crap for the tourists."

"I guess," Stanley agreed. "But I still don't like it."

"Yeah, well just don't chicken out on me. I need you."

"Don't worry, I won't," Stanley assured him, but he was still nervous as hell.

Once they got back to the frat, Peck had convinced Stanley that he had seen either a bear or a moose. It had to be one of those.

SIX

"This guy Peck is a real dick. You know that, right?" Katie told Pierce when he picked her up after work two days after their last camping trip.

"Yeah, I do. But what did he do to piss you off?"

"What did he do?" she asked incredulously. "Have you been reading his Facebook or Twitter pages?"

"Nope. I've blocked him. Why"

"Last night he suggested a 'summer reading list' for you—Steven King's *The Girl Who Loved Tom Bradley* and Rick Hautala's *Little Brothers* and *Untgicahunk,* and he mentioned Bigfoot, but he called it a Pomoola.

"I know who King is," Katie told him. Everybody knows who King is, but I didn't know about this Rick Hautala. I looked him up on Wikipedia. He was another horror writer from UMaine. He graduated in 1974. The *Little Brothers* and *Untgicahunk* books are about …"

"I know who Rick Hautala is … was," Pierce said. He passed away a few years ago. People called him the "other horror writer from Maine." The *Little Brothers* and *Untgicahunk* books were about little, human-like creatures that emerged from underground every five years to dine on human flesh. He was a great writer, but he was a *fiction* writer. He made the little brothers up. They were a product of his imagination. Hell, Peck should have thrown in the *Mountain King,* that's about a Bigfoot monster."

"Of course they were fiction, I know that, but he's trying to spook you. *The Girl Who Loved Tom Bradley* is about a girl lost in the woods. The little brothers and the Pomoola inhabit the

Maine woods. He's trying to get into your head."

"Don't worry—he's not going to spook me. He's just doing it to keep people interested in the challenge and get himself a lot of followers."

"Well, he's doing a good job of it. He gets tons of replies for every post he puts out there. Half of the people are rooting for you and the other half say you'll never be able to do it."

"Really?"

"Yes, really. And you've got quite a fan club among the women. Half of them want to go with you to keep you company."

"Really? Maybe I'll have to unblock him and find out who they are."

That earned him a dirty look, followed by, "If anyone's going to keep you company on this trip, it'll be me."

"I wish you could," he answered.

Peck logged onto Facebook and posted his latest entry on his countdown to Chambers' upcoming trip to the wilds of northern Maine. He also posted a picture of the Bigfoot in the museum. He would add one to each of his subsequent posts. Some were full-size, some were close-ups of various parts of the Bigfoots body.

I just got back from scouting out possible locations for Pierce Chambers' summer adventure. I think I've found the perfect spot for it. It's on a lake, so it has all the fresh water he could want. I did see a few bears in the area, but I'm sure old Survivor Boy can handle them. I didn't see a Pomoola—that's what they call Bigfoot up here—but he's been rumored to be in the area. I guess Pierce could always use the bow and arrows he's taking with him for protection if he needs it.

Then he logged onto Twitter and was pleased to see he had cracked the thousand followers mark. *#Survivorboysadventure: LMAO. Bears in the area where Chambers will be camping. Hope they're friendly!*

His next post was: *#Survivorboysadventure: Bigfoot's up there too, but they call it Pomoola. Maybe Chambers will see one. Maybe he could get himself a new girlfriend. How would all you ladies like that?*

Both posts elicited comments almost immediately. The first

came back from Tim Skully—*The big pussy will probably wet his pants and tap out at the first sign of a bear.*

Ya think? Peck replied.

I'd bet on it, Skully answered.

Tim Skully was actually Derick Stanley. The post had been planned to generate conflict. It worked. Within minutes the flame war was on with Chambers' supporters and detractors chiming in on both sides.

He already had tomorrow's post drafted … Since some of you are sure he'll make it, and some of you are sure he won't, let's have a contest. If you don't think he'll make it, predict the date and time he'll tap out and the reason why. If you think he'll make it, just say so. I'll post the results of the survey next week.

"Did you unblock him yet?" Katie asked after she read the post about the contest.

"No, why?"

"He's running a contest now with people predicting whether you'll make it or not. If not, they have to predict when you'll tap out. And they have to say why they think you'll make it or quit."

"Really? Who's winning? *Make it* or *quit*?"

"Right now … it looks like a toss-up."

That surprised him. "All right, I'll unblock him and see what people are saying."

SEVEN

Peck met Stanley at seven in the morning in front of the frat house three days before he was scheduled to meet Chambers.

"You ready for this?" Peck asked.

Stanley looked at the pickup with the ATV loaded onto a trailer hooked to the back. A second, smaller trailer was in the bed of the pickup. "You bet. You got all the stuff?"

"Of course. Get in and let's go. It's a long ride."

"Okay, but I want to stop for a real breakfast, not McDonald's."

"Fine," Peck agreed, sounding a bit aggravated. But, he had to admit, a real breakfast sounded good.

"There it is," Peck said when he saw the gate guarding the old logging road that led to the spot he had picked out for Chambers to spend his thirty-one days alone.

"When he sees the No Trespassing sign on it he'll have a fit." Stanley told him.

Peck held up a pair of wire cutters. "Don't worry, he won't see it."

"You're going to take the sign down?"

"Just until I get Chambers out in the woods. Then I'll put it back up. That should make sure nobody bothers us."

Just like the last time, Peck kept driving for another mile before pulling into a wide spot on the shoulder of the road so no one would suspect they were in there.

When the trailer was loaded with everything they needed for their camp, Peck drove back to the gate blocking access to the old logging road and once again drove around it.

"We'll go to our campsite and get set up."

The trip to the campsite took over an hour on the ATV. Even though they had cleared it of larger obstacles the first time they were here, it was still slow going in places where the old road had been washed out. "Here's our turnoff," he told Stanley when they reached a branching road that was in even worse shape than the one they were on. It showed signs of recent use. Peck drove until they reached the open area under a stand of pines. "Here we are. From here we should be able to reach him without any problems."

Stanley climbed off the ATV as soon as it came to a stop and staggered for the first few steps. Peck had to stop himself from laughing. When Stanley saw him smiling, he made an effort to stand up straight. "Damn, my back is killing me. How can you stand to ride those things?"

"It's better in the driver's seat. I have the steering wheel to hold onto and I can see what's coming. Now let's unload this stuff and get set up. I want to lie down."

"You going back tonight?" Stanley asked when they had finished setting up their camp.

"Hell, no. It's too late. I'll sleep here tonight and I'll head back early in the morning. I don't have to meet Chambers until the day after tomorrow, so I'll have all day to get home. I still won't make it until late, but that's okay. You'll have to wait here with the stuff until I get back."

Peck left at ten the next morning. Stanley watched him drive away, and then stood listening to the sound of the ATV slowly fade until it was nothing but a memory. That's when the realization that he was all alone out here in the woods struck him. Unlike Peck and Chambers, he had never been much of the outdoors type. In fact, this was the first time he had ever been "camping," as everyone called it.

What the hell was Chambers thinking. Why would anyone want to stay out here alone for a month? Mike's only been gone fifteen minutes and this place is already creeping me out. I'm going back in the tent.

Sitting in the tent proved to be no better. Every sound from outside had him thinking a bear or moose was stomping through the campsite. He refused to even think it might be a Bigfoot. Finally, when he couldn't stand the suspense any longer, he fled the tent. Outside he could at least see what was making the noises.

At first all he heard was the wind, but then a commotion in the woods scared the hell out of him. Something big was out there, he was sure of it. He felt like a complete idiot when it turned out to be two small red squirrels chasing each other up and down a nearby pine tree.

The longer he sat outside the tent, the more comfortable he became with the sounds of the woods. The call of a nuthatch, the rustling of squirrels and chipmunks, the knocking of a woodpecker somewhere in the distance. All these things might have spooked him if he had been hiding from them inside the tent. He was actually starting to enjoy them when the woods went deathly silent. Nothing moved. No birds called, no squirrels or chipmunks scampered through the leaves or up and down trees. Only the sound of the wind remained constant. Then the strident call of a blue jay broke the silence. Soon it was joined by others moving through the trees toward him. *Run! Run!* they seemed to say. But he had nowhere to run. Then he got the distinct feeling something was watching him from the woods. He peered into the trees, but saw nothing. Goosebumps rose on his neck and arms and he retreated back inside the tent.

EIGHT

Pierce messaged Peck the night before they were supposed to meet. *I'll be at the frat house tomorrow at ten if you're still on for this. I'll be bringing all my gear and a friend. You can check out what I'm bringing and I'll check out what you're providing. Once we're both satisfied, we can head to wherever it is you've picked out for my adventure.*

Peck answered almost immediately. *No friends. You're doing this on your own. That's part of the challenge.*

"Screw him," Katie said when she saw Peck's answer.

Don't worry, she's just driving me up there and then to wherever it is we're going. Then she'll come back home. I don't have my own car, and even if I did I wouldn't leave it parked somewhere for a month, and I'm sure as hell not driving up there with you. Besides, I want someone else besides you to know where I am just in case something happens to you while I'm out in the woods.

No friends Peck messaged back.

Then fuck you, the bet's off. And I'll tell everyone on Facebook and Twitter why.

Pierce waited for Peck's reply, almost wishing the trip would be called off. He really didn't want to spend a month in the woods without Katie. He had seen her every day since graduating and couldn't imagine a month without her.

"Good, let's hope he cancels this whole thing," Katie said as they waited for Peck's reply. It came a few minutes later. *Fine, meet me there tomorrow at ten.*

"Oh, well. I guess you're going to do this, aren't you?" she said when Pierce closed the window on his phone.

"I have to. I've come too far to walk away from it now. I'd regret it for the rest of my life."

"I know," she agreed before kissing him and dragging him down on his bed.

"My folks are downstairs," he protested.

""I know," she whispered before letting him go and sitting up. "Come back with me to my house. My parents are gone for the weekend."

"Okay, but first we have to pack everything. I want to leave early so we have time to stop for breakfast. A big one. That's a luxury I won't be having for a while."

When they got to the frat house the next morning, Peck was waiting for them in a pickup truck with an SUV on a trailer behind it. He got out of the pickup when Pierce and Katie pulled up and parked behind him. As soon as Katie saw him, she started laughing.

"What's so funny?" Pierce asked.

"I've been thinking of him as 'pecker head.' Now I think I'll just call him the 'little pecker head.'"

Pierce chuckled, "Yeah, a lot of people call him that. He hates it."

"Mike, this is my girlfriend, Katie Peters," Pierce told Peck once they were all out of their vehicles. "She'll be going with us to see where we're going."

Peck didn't say "Hi," or "Glad to meet you." He just stared at Katie and then nodded. "You have a GPS?" he asked.

For an answer, Pierce held up his phone. "Of course."

Peck handed him a piece of paper with an address printed on it. "Here's where we're going. We won't get there until this afternoon, so we'd better get started. Once we get there. You can follow me to the drop-off point." Then he got back into his pickup and drove off, leaving them staring at his tail lights.

"Asshole," Katie said as she watched him drive away. Pierce had to agree.

On the ride north, Katie had some good advice for Pierce. "If it takes us all day to get there, I think you should wait until tomorrow morning to start. You don't want to get dropped off in the woods somewhere and not have time to look around or set up some kind of camp. Peck would love that. Plus, you want to make sure he has everything he's supposed to have. I can imagine him dropping you off and leaving you there and then you find out half the stuff he promised to bring is missing."

"Good idea," Pierce agreed. "Text him and tell him that. Tell him we'll meet him tomorrow morning at ten."

Katie did and waited for Peck's answer. It came back within minutes.

Fine, but you'd better not be fucking with me. If you don't show up I'm going to post it all over the internet.

"Asshole. Tell him not to worry. I'll be there." Pierce told her.

"Screw him. Let him worry," Katie answered.

Peck pounded the steering wheel and screamed in frustration. This was not going the way he wanted it to. First Chambers shows up with a drop-dead, beautiful redhead, the kind of girl he would never have a chance with. She was tall, at least five nine, had beautiful red hair that came down past her shoulders, brilliant green eyes, a sprinkle of freckles. On top of all that, she had a trim, athletic-looking body to die for.

He had seen the contempt in the bitch's eyes when she looked at him. Now he was going to have to wait until morning to drop Chambers off in the woods. He had wanted to abandon him there in the fucking dark. Now he either needed to find a place to stay, or sleep in the woods with Derick. *Fuck it. I'll find a motel. I'll explain it to Stanley tomorrow.*

Peck saw the Vacancy sign lit up outside the Maple Inn and swung into the parking lot. He was still an hour from his destination, but the area was already getting pretty isolated. He couldn't remember if there was another motel on his route, so he pulled in, intending to get a room.

Peck started to walk toward the motel's office and realized that staying there would not be a good idea. He had all of Chambers' gear in the back of his pickup, plus the ATV and its trailer. If he left it sitting outside a motel up here in the boonies it might just get up and walk away during the night. That's all he needed, to have Chambers show up and then have to tell him the deal was off because he lost all the gear. Reluctantly, he got back into the pickup and kept driving.

By the time Peck got to the old logging road he was absolutely furious. The unfairness of it all ate at him. He was going to have to either sleep in his pickup, or unload everything and load it into the ATV's trailer—leaving it out here would be as bad as leaving it in a motel parking lot—and then drive the ATV to the campsite he and Stanley had set up. It meant he'd have to leave the pickup here. In the end he elected to drive to the campsite. That way, he could at least sleep on a cot with an air mattress and have breakfast in the morning.

The sun was just going down when Peck rolled into the campsite. Stanley was sitting outside the tent in a folding chair waiting for him. "So, did you drop him off? Are we going to fuck with him tonight?"

"No, I have to go back for him tomorrow."

"What happened?"

"He refused to come out this late at night. I can't blame him for that, though. I would have done the same thing."

"So where is he?"

"They said they were going to find a motel and meet me in the morning."

"They? He's supposed to be alone."

"Yeah, well he's not. He brought his girlfriend along to see where he's going. She'll drive home as soon as she does that. Don't worry; he'll be alone when I drop him off at the lake."

Peck lay in the dark fuming. *I'm stuck here in the middle of the woods with Stanley, and Chambers is in some motel banging that redhead. Well, fuck him. Tomorrow he's mine.*

He woke to the sound of the alarm on his phone at eight the next morning. What sunlight managed to make it through the pines lit the inside of the tent. Unlike Pierce and Katie's two-person tent, this one was a six-person model that was ten feet long by ten feet wide with a peak height of seven feet. There was room inside for two folding cots with mattresses and plenty of room for storage. They could bring the folding chairs and table in from outside and set them up between them if it rained. One of them would be in camp every day. Sometimes they would both be there.

Peck could smell coffee and bacon drifting in through the screened window. Stanley was making breakfast. Peck climbed out of his sleeping bag, dressed, and went outside to join him. He wolfed down a plate of scrambled eggs and bacon and grabbed a quick cup of coffee. "I'll be back later. I want to be waiting when Chambers gets there. I wouldn't want him to arrive before me and see me coming from the wrong direction."

The drive back to the drop-off point took just over an hour. Then it was a twenty minute drive to the General Store where he was meeting Chambers. He was early, and there was no sign of the prick and his girlfriend, so he got a coffee and a donut and sat in the pickup and waited for them.

NINE

Pierce and Katie pulled into the Maple Inn a half hour after Peck had pulled out. The GPS told them it was still an hour from the rendezvous point. The only reason Peck had beat them there was that they had stopped to have lunch.

"Wait here, I'll get us a room," Pierce told her.

"Oh, yes, lord and master," she answered with a smile. "See if they have a queen-size bed. You take up too much room in a full-size."

"Yes, ma'am."

When he came back, he had a key to unit 12. It was the last one on the end.

"Queen-size, just like you requested, and I got the number of a pizza place that delivers," he told her when he climbed behind the wheel.

"Good man. Now let's go find that room."

Once they were there, Katie flopped on the bed and smiled at him. "So, how hungry are you?"

"Not *that* hungry," he told her and jumped on the bed with her.

When they finally got around to ordering dinner, Katie told him to order two large, meat lovers pizzas.

"Two? We'll never eat two whole pizzas."

"Then we'll have leftovers. This is the last dinner you're going to get without foraging for it. You need to eat what you can now."

"Right," he agreed, and made the call.

The pizzas, along with a quart bottle of coke, arrived thirty minutes later. Pierce paid the delivery guy and gave him a five buck tip. When the man handed over the pies, he looked past Pierce to where Katie was sitting on the bed. He tried not to stare, but he did. Pierce just grinned at him and closed the door.

They made love once more before going to sleep and again in the morning. Then Pierce took the last shower he was going to get for a month. They walked out the door of the Maple Inn the same time Peck left Stanley and headed for their meeting point. If they hadn't stopped for breakfast, they would have arrived there before him.

"Eat the sandwich," Katie told him as they drove toward their meeting with Peck.

"I just had a bacon and cheese omelet, sausage and home fries. How do you expect me to eat an egg and cheese sandwich on a hard roll? If I eat it, I'm going to puke and I don't need that."

"Okay, don't" she finally agreed after another five minutes of trying to get him to eat it.

They rode in silence for the last half hour of the trip. Neither one wanted to talk about his upcoming departure. Ten miles from the meeting point Katie yelped "Watch out!" At the same time she yelled, Pierce was hitting the brakes and swerving to avoid a black bear that darted across the road.

"Stop the car," she demanded. "I don't want you to do this. It's too dangerous. Let's just go tell Peck to fuck off and go home."

"I can't. I'd never be able to look myself in the mirror if I did. I at least have to try."

"Then promise me you'll bail out if it gets dangerous."

"I will. I promise."

"There he is," Katie announced when they pulled into the parking lot of the General Store. Peck was parked to one side next to a pay telephone booth.

When they drove up, Peck refused to get out of the truck, so Pierce and Katie got out and went to him.

"You see all the Bigfoot signs on the way here?" Peck asked, referring to the signs to visit the Bigfoot Museum in Tinkers Falls.

"We saw them. Typical tourist trap. Bigfoot's not real." Katie replied.

"Maybe, maybe not," Peck answered. "I guess he'll find out."

"Cut the crap, and let's get going," Pierce told him.

"You that anxious to get started? Fine, follow me."

Five miles from the General Store Peck turned off onto a dirt and gravel road. The trailer carrying the ATV bounced on the uneven surface and kicked up a rooster tail of dust that coated Pierce's windshield to the point he had to use the wipers to be able to see.

"I'll bet that asshole's enjoying this," Katie said as dust coated the car.

Pierce didn't answer; he just fell back a half mile to let most of the dust settle before he had to drive through it.

When Peck finally braked to a stop, it was beside a locked gate that barred entry to an old logging road. He was out of his pickup and working on unloading the ATV when they pulled up.

"Load your stuff up and let's go," he said once the ATV was off the trailer.

"Not so fast," Katie told him. "We want to go over what you brought to make sure everything's there."

"Fine, and I want to see what he brought, to make sure he doesn't have anything he's not supposed to have."

After they had all gone through all the gear and loaded it onto the trailer, Peck climbed onto the ATV and told Pierce to get in next him. "Unless you want to walk," he said.

"Just a minute," Katie told him and went back to the car. When she came back she handed Pierce the egg and cheese sandwich. "Eat this and then make sure the phone works before you leave."

"He can't eat that. From now on he has to find all his own food."

"Screw you. That shit starts once you drop him off," Katie snapped back.

Katie grabbed Pierce's arm as he was climbing onto the seat beside Peck. "Wait, try that satellite phone. Make sure it works before you leave."

Pierce nodded and dug the satellite phone out of his pack

where he had stowed it. "You have service?" he asked her.

Katie checked her phone and frowned. "Nope, try calling home."

Pierce did and got the answering machine.

"Let's go, Chambers. I want to get back in time for dinner and it's a long way to where I'm dropping you off."

"Hang on a minute," Pierce told him and handed Katie one of the cameras. "Film this. Keep it going for about ten yards after we start. Then I'll come back for the camera."

She waited for Peck to drive the ATV through the underbrush and around the locked gate before she started filming.

"Well, I'm off. Wish me luck," Pierce told the camera before climbing on to the seat next to Peck.

"Stop," Pierce said after they had gone twenty yards. Once Peck did, Pierce hopped off the ATV and ran back to retrieve the camera.

"Okay, I'll see you here in a month," Katie told him over the gate. Then she gave him a hug and a kiss and watched as they drove away. Everything Pierce was going to have to rely on to live in the wild was stacked behind them on the trailer behind the ATV. Katie didn't start crying until they were out of sight.

PART TWO

INTO THE WILD

Day 1

The ride along the old logging road was anything but smooth. Pierce managed to film some of it but gave up because he had to hold onto the ATV to keep from being thrown out. "How long will it take us to get there?" he asked after they had bounced along for ten minutes.

"Relax, Chambers. It's going to be an hour at least."

Pierce shut up and started paying attention to the environment they were riding through. He was amazed at how quickly the woods seemed to engulf them. At places the trees crowded right up to the edge of the trail they were on. At others they retreated, only to be replaced by thick underbrush. Hardwoods alternated with stands of pines. He tried to identify as many edible plants that he could along the way. This was a far cry from the well-tended and open campsites he had shared with Katie, and he was starting to wonder if he had bitten off more than he could chew.

Occasionally, overgrown side paths, once logging trails like the one they were on, branched off to disappear into the forest. One in particular piqued his interest. He wouldn't have paid it any mind, except that it had been covered over with branches, as if someone had intentionally blocked it off. The grass and weeds beyond the makeshift barricade had been crushed and pushed aside. Someone had been on it recently. Perhaps Peck, looking for a place to leave him? But why try to hide it?

When Peck finally stopped the ATV at the edge of a marsh, they were a mile from the barricaded logging trail. "We're here. Unload your gear and I'm out of here."

Peck made no effort to help unload. Instead, he sat and

smirked while Pierce moved everything from the back of the
ATV to the ground. As soon as the last piece was off, Peck made
a U-turn through the brush, leaving a path of crushed vegetation
in his wake.

"I'll pick you up right here in a month … if you can make it,"
he called as he gunned the ATV back toward his pickup. Pierce
just managed to catch the ATV on the camera before it disappeared down the trail. He could still hear it, but within minutes
even that faded. He had watched Peck go with mixed emotions.
He was glad to be done with the asshole, but his link to the outside world was gone. He was truly alone in the wilderness. He
slowly turned in a complete circle and all he saw was woods,
the lake, an empty sky, and marsh. The enormity of what he was
about to attempt finally hit him. He would be completely on his
own out here for the next thirty-one days.

Once he managed to shake off his sudden case of nerves,
Pierce made his way to the pile of gear. He was tempted to go
through it, but his first priority had to be shelter and a fire. He
was about to set off to find a good spot to set up camp when he
remembered he had to set the camera up first. Rules were rules
after all, and he had to stick to them. It wouldn't do to make it
through the entire thirty-one days only to find out he fucked
up and disqualified himself by not following the rules they had
agreed on. And just in case he forgot the rules, they were encased
for him in a laminated sheet he could always refer to.

Rule 1: Record at least two hours of activity every day.
Rule 2: Narrate all recordings.
Rule 3: Drama and suspense are the name of the game. Ensure
you have some every day.
Rule 4: Only use the emergency beacon in a true emergency.
Minor injuries do not constitute an emergency.
Rule 5: Failure to complete the entire thirty-one days constitutes
failure. All royalties and rewards are forfeit.

Before setting off to find a campsite, he went to the waterproof, shockproof, aluminum trunk that contained the cameras,
spare batteries and tripods he was going to use to record his

thirty-one days of solitude. He wasn't supposed to use the trunk for anything other than storage for the cameras and they had to be returned there anytime they were not in use.

The trunk contained three cameras, a tripod, two sets of *magic arms* camera mounts, and spare batteries. The cameras recorded straight to internal memory so there was no need for film packs.

Pierce set one of the cameras up on a tripod to record his location and the pile of gear sitting in the middle of the old logging road. Once he had the camera positioned like he wanted, he turned it on and walked into the shot.

"Okay, I'm on my own, alone, in the north woods of Maine. Let me show you my gear and where I am." Then he picked up the camera and panned it in a three-hundred-sixty-degree circle, starting with the old logging road.

"Here's the road, if you can call it a road, that I came in on. The trip took a little over an hour by ATV. I have no idea how far we came." Then he slowly turned in a circle, describing the rest of the area. After he was done with that, he turned to the pile of gear. "I'm not going to go over this now. You'll see it all eventually. Right now I'm going to find a place to set up camp. I want to get away from this marsh. Come nighttime the mosquitoes are going to be out in force.

"There's jewelweed along the edge of the marsh, and there are plenty of cattails. Carbs aren't going to be a problem. My biggest challenge will be protein. But that's for later, after I'm settled. My girlfriend, Katie, made me eat enough this morning to get me through today.

"What I want is a shelter that will protect me from the rain and wind. Hopefully, I can find something like that. Something I can augment with the tarp I'm supposed to use for a tent."

In the next two hours he located a large deadfall where the exposed roots could be used for the back of a shelter. He also found a rock ledge with a five-foot overhang. The overhang was about eight feet wide, six feet high and five feet deep. Once he was satisfied that he had found his campsite, he went back to his pile of gear.

"Well, I've found a place to set up camp," he told the camera. "Let's go take a look."

The view bounced and shook as Pierce made his way through the woods to the deadfall. He removed the camera from the magic arm and aimed it at the wall of roots. "This is the first site I considered," he said when he walked into the shot. "I could use the back for the rear of my shelter and drape the tarp over the top to keep out the rain. It's not ideal, and I'd use it if I had to, but luckily I don't. I found something I like better. Let's go take a look at that."

This time he turned the camera off as he made his way to the new site. Woods were woods after all. When he got there, he turned it back on and panned from left to right across the area he had chosen to set up camp. "That rock ledge runs from down there, all the way up to there," he narrated as he moved the camera across it. "And, right here," he said as he walked toward the overhang, "is where I'm going to be living for the next month. It's only about a quarter mile from the lake, so I won't have to go too far for water. The wall in back is solid rock and the overhang will keep me out of the rain. I'll make a lean-to in front of it with the tarp, and I'll have myself a nice, comfy shelter. Now I just have to go and get my stuff." With that, he turned the camera off and headed back to the marsh to collect his gear.

It would take three trips to get everything from the marsh to the new camp. On his first trip he hauled the box of camera gear to the new campsite. Before he left, he set one of the cameras on the tripod and aimed it so it would capture him when he came back for the rest of his equipment. He turned it on just before leaving. It would be filming nothing but the empty woods while he was gone, but he could delete all the empty footage later.

The trip back to the marsh took him over half an hour. As he walked, he talked to the camera he had attached to a magic arm. "Okay, now that I've found my campsite, it's time to move everything. And, I've got to get back and get a fire going before sunset. I don't want to be stuck out here in the wilderness without one."

He continued to narrate all the while he packed his gear into his backpack. When he had stuffed everything into it that he could, he grabbed the bow and arrows and headed back toward his campsite. He'd come back for the rest of it after he dropped this load off.

"Okay, I'm on my way," he said and walked into the woods. The camera he had set up before he left was waiting for him when he arrived. It captured him approaching the rock ledge with the overhang. He walked up to and past it, stopped and repositioned it so it was aiming at the covered space under the overhang. Now it would show him entering the protected space that would become his shelter. "Home, sweet, home," he announced when he set his backpack down. Then he turned the camera off and went back for the rest of his gear.

"Now I need to get a fire going. I've got the overhang for shelter, so I can wait until tomorrow to set up," Pierce told the camera once he had moved everything to his new home.

He didn't bother filming his hunt for firewood; time wouldn't allow it. That could be done later. When he had collected what he needed for the night, he filmed himself clearing out the space under the overhang and making a place for the fire off to one side. When he scraped off the buildup of leaves and moss, he found more of the stone shelf. "This is going to be a great place for a fire," he explained as he worked.

With the camera zoomed in on the site of his prospective fire, Pierce began his narration. "It's almost sundown. I need to get this fire going now. I've already built a stone barrier, now I just have to get it going … if I can."

He placed a pile of tinder and birch-bark shavings on the bare rock and used the ferro rod fire starter to produce a few sparks. "Birch bark is excellent for catching a spark and producing a flame," he explained. His words proved accurate when a small flame appeared after his third try. He then placed the fire starter aside so he could lean in close to the bundle of kindling. He blew gently on it until the flame spread. Then he carefully fed it with twigs he had set aside just for that purpose.

"Success," he said as he smiled into the camera. Anyone watching would have thought he'd been doing it all his life instead of less than a month. *Thank God Katie made me practice this before I came out here. I just wish she could be here to see this.*

"I'll have a bit of warmth and light tonight. I don't have time to make a real shelter, so I'll just wrap myself and my sleeping bag in my tarp tonight to keep out the damp." Then he turned the camera off and waited for sunset.

Pierce turned the camera back on when the sun started to dip below the horizon and the woods started to fill with shadows. "Well, that was close," he commented as he panned the camera from the fire to the darkening forest.

"The temperature's dropping so I'm really glad I got that fire going. I only wish I had something to eat. I thought a big breakfast and the egg and cheese sandwich I had just before I came out here would be plenty, but I guess I was wrong. It's too early to dig into my emergency rations, so I'll have to go hungry tonight. I'll go foraging tomorrow. Right now I'm going to sit by this fire for a while and then try and get some sleep."

As the light faded and the darkness closed in around him, Pierce automatically reached for his phone to see what time it was. When he realized he didn't have it, the fact that he was completely shut off from the rest of the world finally hit him.

Even with a partial moon, the sky was filled with stars—more than he had ever seen, but they were poor company. A breeze rippled the leaves in the trees above him, but it didn't reach the ground. Around him the air felt as still as the grave. At first the silence was only broken by the snap of the logs in the fire, but he slowly became aware of other sounds in the night. There was the far-off croak of bullfrogs from the lake, the hoot of an occasional owl and, once in a while, the haunting call of a loon. Soon even they faded into the background.

Time to get some sleep, he told himself, donning the head lamp to make his way to his sleeping bag under the rock overhang. When he turned it on, instead of a bright beam, all it gave off was a weak, yellow glow. "Fucking Peck," he swore when he realized the batteries were practically dead.

"Well this sucks," he said as he held the head lamp in front of the camera. "I should have checked this before I let Peck leave."

He used what little light it provided to make his way to his sleeping bag before turning it off. *The asshole probably did it on purpose. I'm going to have to save it for emergencies,* he thought as he settled into the bag.

After Peck left Chambers standing in the middle of the old logging road, he made his way back to the campsite he and Stanley were sharing. He had to move the debris he had stacked in front of the side trail, but that only took a few minutes. He was grinning like an idiot when he arrived there. Compared to what Chambers was going to have to put together, he and Stanley would be living in the lap of luxury.

Stanley looked at him and the empty trailer and knew everything had gone as planned.

"How'd it go?" he asked.

"Great. The fool never checked the head lamp. Wait until he tries to use that tonight."

"What now?" Stanley asked.

"Nothing. We'll let him get settled. Tomorrow I'll hike over there and find out where he set up camp. Then we can plan our next moves."

A lump grew in Katie's throat as she watched the ATV motor off into the woods. She had known she was going to miss Pierce, but hadn't realized just how much until he was gone. When the ATV disappeared around a curve, a deep sob shook her. They had talked on the phone or been together every day since he had come home. *What the hell is wrong with me? He's just camping in the woods. If anything goes wrong he can call for help or just walk out.*

Her ride home was filled with thoughts of Pierce and Peck. Peck was an asshole, no doubt about that. She didn't like or trust him. If she knew what he had planned, she never would have let Pierce go.

DAY 2

Pierce woke with the sun. The fire had gone out and he was stiff from sleeping on the ground—not even the ground, really. He hadn't taken the time to make a bed of pine boughs or dead leaves, so he had wound up sleeping on the hard rock shelf under the overhanging ledge. He was already sore from bumping around on the ATV and now his body was also feeling the effects of sleeping on stone.

After he had stretched and relieved himself in the woods, he set up the camera, pointed it at his sleeping area, and started recording his day.

"All I had for padding between me and the hard rock was the bottom of my sleeping bag. My hip feels like someone pummeled me with a baseball bat. That's going to have to change. I'm going to get some bedding in here today to get off that hard stone. But first, I'm going to find something for breakfast. I'm famished. It's been over twenty hours since I've had anything to eat."

At this point he turned off the camera and headed back to the marsh where Peck had dropped him off. Once there, he set the camera up on a tripod facing the cattails and turned it on.

"There it is folks, breakfast. You probably know them as cattails, but did you know you can eat them? It's a little early in the season for the rhizomes, and a bit too late for the shoots." Then he pointed to a long, slender, green part of the plant just above the larger female seed head that would eventually become the brown "cattail" everyone was familiar with. He cut several off with his knife. "But these, these are immature male flowers and they should be fine. They may not look too appetizing, but they're edible.

"That takes care of the carb part of my breakfast, now let's see if I can find some protein," he told the camera as he picked up the bow and arrows and held them out for his audience. "It's a good thing I've been practicing with this. It's a different from the compound bow I've always used. At first it threw me off, now I'm pretty good with it, especially within ten feet or so. I'm going to use the target arrows. There's no need for a hunting arrow for a frog." Then he went off camera, walking along the edge of the bog. He crept along, arrow nocked, looking for a target. He hadn't gone ten feet when he spied a bullfrog. He tried to creep closer, but as soon as he was within what he considered a sure shot, the frog leaped off the bank and into the water with a loud croak. "Damn," he swore,

Within minutes, he spied another one. This time he didn't risk trying to get closer. He took the shot from ten feet away. The arrow found its mark and Pierce rushed to reach the struggling amphibian before it could slip off the arrow.

"That's one," he said to himself before setting off to find more.

The marsh was filled with frogs. Some were too small to consider eating, while others croaked and fled into the water before he could even draw his bow. Several of them sat in in the water with their heads just above the surface and he wouldn't risk losing one of his six arrows by shooting at them. He finally managed to bag two more. The next time he came back, he'd have to try an easier way to hunt them.

As he held the frogs up for the lens, Pierce caught a flicker of movement in the distance. He got the impression of something large. It was there for a second, and then it was gone. Deer? Bear? He didn't know, but hoped it was the former rather than the latter.

"I think I just saw something big moving up there on the road. I hope it was a deer, and not a bear," he said. But I'll worry about that if I see it again. Right now I need some jewelweed for tea.

"Okay, that's it, cattails, frog legs and jewelweed tea for breakfast. I'll get some water from the lake, return to my camp, start a fire and cook these."

Once he was back at his campsite, he set the cattail heads and jewelweed aside and headed to the lake with his two-quart pot and the bullfrogs. He cleaned the frogs using a fallen tree for a cutting board, discarding all but the legs. Those he skinned and placed in the pot which he had already filled with water from the lake. Before he left, he threw the leftover parts in the lake so they wouldn't attract scavengers.

Before turning the camera back on to film cooking his breakfast, he started a fire.

"I need to boil these cattail heads," he said as he put the pot of water on the fire to heat. "Before I do though, I'm going to make jewelweed tea. These," he said, holding up the skinned frog legs, "I'll roast over the fire."

Once he had brought the water to a boil, he realized he couldn't both make tea and boil the cattails at the same time. "Well, this sucks. I don't have anything to drink out of. I can't make tea and boil these cattails," he told the camera. "I guess I'll just have to make the tea later."

He continued filming and talking while he boiled the cattails. He elected to roast the frog legs. "Not your all-American breakfast of bacon and eggs, but a fine meal just the same. I just wish there was more of it, because I'm still hungry," he said when he was done.

"I guess it's time to make a more permanent shelter. The overhang is fine for sleeping, but I need more room. I can't even stand up in it. I'm going to need a ridge pole and several side poles to support my tarp. It'll be like a big pup tent with open sides.

"Look at this," he told the camera as he pointed it at a tree growing in front the overhang. "See that notch about ten feet up the trunk? That would be a perfect cradle for one end of the ridge pole. That's going to be strong and it will save me some work. Now let's go find the poles I'll need."

After using the saw to cut down enough small trees for his needs—one twenty-five-foot ridge pole and six twelve-foot side poles, he was ready to construct his shelter. That's when he realized he had nothing to tie the tarp to the poles with … or the poles to each other for that matter. He thought about using cattail leaves, but then had a better idea. He'd use the thermal underwear. There was no way he'd need those in the middle of the summer. Now he was glad Katie had insisted he bring everything the list allowed.

"Thermal underwear. I don't think I'm going to need these, so I'm going to sacrifice them to make a shelter. The material should last for the time I'm here," he said as he sat in front of the camera cutting the underwear pants into strips. When he finished, he had enough for his needs.

The next step was to tie the ends of two of the poles together. When that was done he hoisted one end of the ridge pole into place into the notch in the tree. He placed the other end in a notch formed by the poles he had tied together. Then he used them to lift the ridge pole. Once that was done, he spread the "feet" of the pole apart and pushed them into the ground. Two ends of the frame for his shelter were now in place. Three more on each side should do it.

"Well, duh!" Pierce said once he had his frame assembled and in place. "I don't have any way to get the tarp over the frame. I'm going to have to take it down, spread the tarp over it and put it back up." This was easier said than done, but he managed it. The result was a twelve-foot-long, pup-tent-like structure open on the sides and both ends. One end was only a foot from the rock overhang.

By the time he had finished, most of the day had already slipped away. He felt proud and satisfied with what he had accomplished but realized he was really hungry and had nothing to eat other than the emergency supplies he had brought with him, and he didn't want to break into them this early in the game.

"One more thing to do before I call it a day. I'm going to get a pot of water from the lake so I'll have it in the morning."

As he panned the camera over his creation, he remarked that he had worked through lunch and that he had nothing for dinner. "I still have time to find something if I hurry, so I'm going back to the marsh," he said before turning the camera off.

Pierce was hoping to score a few more frogs but that wasn't to be. He was about to give up because sunset was only an hour or so away, and he still had things to do back at the shelter, when he saw a three-foot snake slipping through the reeds. He stood still, watching as it made its way toward him. When it was within a few feet of where he stood, he carefully nocked an arrow, drew and fired. He hit the snake just behind its head. He had dinner.

By the time he had returned to his camp, skinned and cleaned his prize, retrieved fresh water from the lake, started a new fire and grilled the snake, it was already getting dark. Without any means of artificial light he was tethered to his campsite until the sun came back up in the morning.

"Here it is, dinner," he said, holding the snake up for the camera. "One of the books I read said snake meat has about half the calories and half the fat of steak, so this is great."

Snake grilled over the fire and jewelweed tea replaced the calories Pierce had burned building his shelter and foraging. But, even after finishing the snake, he was still hungry. He was tempted to boil some rice, but that would mean walking down to the lake to fetch more water. Not a good idea.

As he sat in the growing dark, he automatically reached for his phone. His hand hadn't even reached his pocket before he remembered he didn't have it. The enormity of it hit him again. He was utterly alone here—no phone, no computer and no one to talk to except the camera. He didn't even have a book to read. He had never been this isolated from other people or technology. It was not a comfortable feeling. Needing to talk to someone, he set up the camera and started filming.

"It's only day two and I'm starting to feel the isolation of being out here alone. I'm not sure what I had expected, but this isn't it. Back in civilization, it's hard to find a quiet place where you can spend a few minutes alone. It's just the opposite here. I'm going to have to find some way to occupy my mind, especially at night when I'm stuck here in my camp with nothing to do but feed the fire, stare into the flames, talk to you and think of Katie."

The flames were almost hypnotic as they danced along the branches he fed them and the growing bed of coals beneath them. In his mind's eye, Pierce imagined little flaming sprites that leapt and danced from coals to wood, demanding to be fed. *If I had a computer, or even a pad and pen, I could write a story about that, maybe call it "Feeding the Flames."* He worked the entire thing out in his head, knowing it would be gone in the morning. Oh sure, the idea might be there, some scrap of the tale, but the body of the thing would be gone. He could recreate it, but it would never be the same, and he mourned its passing—a story that would never be told.

A deep chuffing sound brought Pierce out of his reverie. He waited, not really sure he had heard anything. Then it came again, from somewhere above and behind him. He wasn't sure, but he thought it might be a bear. *"Oh, shit. Stay away buddy, stay away. Nothing here for you,"* he whispered, needing to hear the sound of his own voice. Then, remembering what the contestants on the show did, called out "Hey bear. Hey bear," hoping the sound of a human voice would scare it away.

Pierce waited, listening to see if calling out had done any good. He heard something moving in the dark. Twigs snapped and several grunts split the silence. Then it seemed to be moving away. The whole episode only lasted a few minutes, but it would stay with him, keeping him awake well into the night.

"I'm going to find where he made his camp. You stay here and keep an eye on things. If anyone comes, just tell them we're camping out here for a few days," Peck told Stanley over a breakfast of cold cereal, fresh strawberries and coffee.

"Okay. How long do you think you'll be?"

"As long as it takes. What did you think?"

Stanley shrugged, "Shit, I don't know, but it shouldn't take all day."

"You worried?"

"Nah, it's just pretty boring out here alone." He didn't want Peck laughing at him, so he didn't mention the feeling he had had about being watched from the woods.

"That's the idea," Peck told him.

Peck took the ATV but stopped well before where he had dropped Chambers off. He could walk the rest of the way. He approached the marsh with caution, taking care to keep out of sight of the place he had left Chambers. He doubted he would make his camp there, but you never knew. When he reached a spot on the road where he could see the marsh, he used the binoculars he had brought for any sign of his adversary. The prick wasn't there, so Peck started walking again. As soon as he did, Chambers appeared out of the marsh. Peck immediately jumped back into the bushes, praying Chambers hadn't seen him.

He waited until he thought it was safe to peek out before raising the binoculars to his eyes and looking to see what Chambers was doing. He was just in time to see him step off the road. *Good, he's heading back to his camp. Now I know where to look.*

"That was fast. Did you find him?" Stanley asked when Peck got back to their camp.

"No, but I know where to look. I'm going back out tonight. I don't want to take a chance of him seeing me when I'm out there looking for him."

"So what are we going to do for the rest of the day?" Stanley asked.

"We're going to town to have lunch and do some shopping. We need more cereal, fruit and milk. We'll also bring back grinders for dinner."

"Aren't you worried he'll hear the ATV?"

"Nope. He's off to the right of the road, we're off to the left. We're far away enough that the sound of the ATV will never reach him."

"Great. Let's get going then. I'm getting sick of these woods."

The trip back to the pickup and then into the nearest town took almost two hours. That left them only an hour to eat, get their supplies and grinders, and be back on the road. Peck worried about the ATV the entire time they were gone. He had parked it far enough into the woods that it couldn't be seen from the end of the road, but it still worried him to the point that he decided only one of them would stay at the campsite at a time.

"We can't leave the pickup parked out here while we're out in the woods. It's a sure sign we're trespassing out there. Someone's going to report it to the cops."

"Why would they do that?" Stanley asked.

"Because it's posted. Remember the No Trespassing sign we took down?"

"Oh yeah. So what do you suggest?"

"One of us will have to stay at that motel."

"Are you crazy? That's expensive. It's July, for Christ's sake. I don't have that kind of money. Do you?"

Peck had to admit he didn't, but the idea of leaving the ATV or the pickup sitting out there in the woods ate at him. "I'll think of something else," he finally said, but by the time they got back to the old logging road he still hadn't come up with a better idea.

Peck waited until full dark before he went looking for Chambers. The ATV's headlights lit up the trail in front of him, but he still had to creep along at not much more than the pace of a brisk walk. Without the benefit of the night-vision glasses Peck had with him, Chambers would be stuck in his shelter until morning. He drove the ATV as far as he had that afternoon, then donned the night-vision glasses and went on foot from there. When he got to the point where he had seen Chambers leave the road and enter the woods, he did the same.

He picked his way through the woods until he saw the flickering light of Chambers' fire. *Got you*, he thought and slowly made his way toward it, being careful not to make any noise. There would be plenty of time for that later, after he got a good look at Chambers' camp.

As he crept closer, the light from the fire overwhelmed everything else. He could make out Chambers sitting near it, but not much more. He looked left and right of the fire, trying to eliminate some of its glare and got feel for the camp. He'd get a better idea of what was there when he observed in daylight, so he backed off and started to circle around behind it.

He hadn't gone far when he ran into the rock ledge. He followed it nearly to the logging road before coming to a point where it dropped back to ground level and disappeared into the forest floor. Walking the ridge, he made his way back to the site of Chambers' camp. He could tell when he arrived there by the firelight reflected off the trees. He was about twenty feet above the asshole.

Perfect, he thought and went about staging the scene. He set up the small speaker he had brought in a backpack and connected it to his iPhone. *Here you go, Survivor Boy, let's see how you like this.* Then he sent the recorded grunts of a black bear into the night. He shuffled around in the dead leaves covering the forest floor, broke off a few branches and snagged a bit of bear hair on another. He played the recorded bear noises one more time before he left.

Peck had been gone for nearly two hours when Stanley heard something shuffling around outside the tent. He got the impression it was something big.

What the hell is that? Something's out there. He considered looking outside, but then thought better of it. *What if it's a bear? God, I hope not.*

The noise only lasted for a few minutes, and then the night fell silent. Ten minutes later he heard the sound of the ATV returning. *Asshole. It was him. Very funny. Well, I'm not going to let him know he spooked me.*

"How'd it go? Did you find him?" he asked when Peck came into the tent.

"Oh yeah. It's perfect. He's right up against a rock ledge. I got above him where he couldn't see me. I played the bear sounds and made enough noise shuffling around that he couldn't help hear it."

"What did he do?"

"Called out 'Hey bear. Hey bear,' like they do on the show, but he sounded nervous as hell. I had to keep from laughing. He must have been shaking in his boots down there."

"Now what?"

"Now we get some sleep. See you in the morning."

Stanley tried, but the noise he had heard before Peck returned ran around in his head like a mouse in the walls. What if it hadn't been Mike?

DAY 3

Pierce woke at sunrise after a restless, if less painful night's sleep. The first thing on his mind was food. The snake had been a lucky score, but he couldn't count on luck, and had to find enough to eat every day if he was going to make up for the calories he was burning. He could see why candidates on the reality show all lost weight while they were in the wild. He felt like he had already dropped a few pounds.

"I need to find more to eat today than I did yesterday," he told the camera. "My best chance for that is the lake. It should be filled with fish. But to catch them, I'm going to need bait. I wish I would have saved some of the snake or frogs. I could have used a bit of them. I won't make that mistake again. Now I'm going to have to find something else. I saw a rotting log yesterday. Maybe I can find some grubs or beetles there."

"Here it is," he said when he got there. "Let's see if I'm going to get lucky."

After he set the camera up to film his efforts, he used his knife to strip the bark off the rotting trunk. It took a few minutes, but he found a large white grub of some kind squirming in the soft wood.

"Bait ... or breakfast," he said, picking it up and holding it in front of the lens. "Hah, just kidding, I'm not that hungry yet." Then he went back to searching for more. He stopped when he had three of them.

"Now, let's go catch some breakfast," he said, holding up his spool of fishing line and hooks.

Pierce made a bobber from a dry stick, set it at six feet above the hook and threw it as far as he could out into the lake. His first bite came almost immediately. He waited for the stick to disappear and then yanked on the line to set the hook. A few minutes later he was holding a six-inch yellow perch up to the camera. Ten minutes later, two more had joined the first one on the bank.

"Well, it doesn't look like I'm going to starve today," he said and turned the camera off.

Pierce had way too much to do today, so instead of foraging for carbs to go with the fish, he dug into his supply of rice. He didn't tell the camera that.

After he had eaten, he took the camera and saw and headed into the woods. "Today is a firewood day. I need enough dry wood to keep the fire going if rains. I think I can get it at the deadfall I found. You remember, the one I said I could have used for a camp if I hadn't found the overhang."

It took him most of the day to gather the wood he needed and carry it back to his campsite where he stacked it under the safety of the tarp. He filmed part of cutting it and carrying it just to show his audience.

"This one," he said holding up one of the larger pieces, "is going to be my chair. I'm getting tired of sitting on the ground. Now let's see if I can catch a few perch for dinner."

He was about to leave when a peal of thunder rolled in the distance.

"You hear that? It looks like I got that wood in just in time, but it means I'm going to go hungry tonight. Maybe I can at least get some more bedding before it starts raining." Before he could, the first raindrops hit. They were big, heavy drops that sounded like pebbles landing on the tarp. Soon they were tapping out a rhythm that promised some serious rain was on its way. Unless he wanted to get drenched, he was stuck in camp until morning.

"I've been thinking about it," Peck said over breakfast. "We can't leave the pickup parked out there at the end of the logging road. If someone sees it there day after day they're either going to steal it, vandalize it, or report it to the police. We can't afford for any of those things to happen."

"So what do you want to do?" Stanley asked.

"We're going to stay out here in shifts. I'll drive you back to the truck and you can go get a room at the motel. I've got plenty of food for now, so you can come back in three days. Be at the parking spot at noon and we'll swap places. Then I can take a day off. How's that sound to you?"

"Okay, I guess. But are you sure you'll only want one day off?"

"Yeah, I want to be here to fuck with Chambers. Now help me put everything inside the tent, then I'll take you out to the pickup."

"How are we going to pay for it? You solve that problem yet?"

"Yeah, I still have some money left from the GoFundMe account. Then, when Peck bails, I'll sell the gear to pay for the rest. You have a credit card you can use?"

Stanley twisted uncomfortably before answering. "Yeah, as long as you promise to pay me back."

"No problem," Peck assured him.

Peck stopped just out of sight of the gate that blocked the logging road from the dirt road where the pickup was parked. "I'll meet you back here at noon, three days from now. Bring back enough food for a couple of days. I'll pick up more once I know what we need when I go into town for the day."

"Okay," Stanley agreed.

"Well, what are you waiting for ... go," Peck said when Stanley stood there looking at him.

"Keys," Stanley answered, sticking out his hand for them.

"Right," Peck agreed, and handed them over.

Halfway back to his camp Peck heard the rumble of distant thunder "Shit," he swore as the sky darkened in the west. He was still a good forty-five minutes from the tent and he didn't think he had time to get there before the rain hit. He was right: twenty minutes later the sky opened up. He was soaked to the skin and shivering within minutes. "Fuckin' rain," he swore and kept driving.

By the time he reached the tent he was totally miserable. *At least we brought everything inside, before we left,* he thought when he stopped the ATV and made his way to the tent where he unzipped the door and stepped inside. He stripped off his clothes and wrapped himself in Stanley's sleeping bag. There was no way he was going to use his own. He had to sleep in that tonight. *I hope that fucking Chambers is as miserable as I am*, he thought as he waited to stop shivering.

When he was warm enough and dry enough, he climbed out of the sleeping bag and dressed in clean clothes. Then he lit the lantern and went about setting up the inside of the tent. When he was done he had the table and one chair set up in the middle. The lantern and the propane stove sat on it. The stove had two burners and a grill. He unzipped one of the windows to provide some ventilation before turning everything on. The flames were soon throwing heat into tent. Then he put on a pot of coffee and went about making a dinner of beans and franks.

Even though the sun hadn't set yet, it was dark outside when he finished eating. It was still raining, so even if it stopped he knew he wouldn't be making the trip over to Chambers' camp. No, he'd stay here, warm and dry, with a good book, music on his iPhone, and a bottle of apricot brandy.

Fuck you, Chambers. Suffer, he thought as he the settled in for the night. He wasn't aware that from outside, the light created shadows on the tent wall that revealed his every move to the eyes that were watching from the dark.

Pierce sat under the tarp wearing the rain jacket and trousers. It was damp and chilly enough that he needed them. The fire provided enough heat and light to keep the night at bay, but did nothing to relieve the boredom or sense of loneliness he felt. The rain drumming above him on the tarp added to the gloom of the surrounding woods. Normally, he loved the sound of rain in the night, but tonight it reminded him of the first night he had spent with Katie. He tried not to think about her, but the more he tried not to, the more she dominated his thoughts.

Fuck you, Peck. I never would have agreed to this if I knew how much I was going to miss Katie. I'm tempted to tap out now just to get back to her. I would if we hadn't spent so much time preparing for this. She expects me to make it, so I will.

His thoughts slowly shifted from Katie to Rick Hautala's little brothers. He knew they were just a figment of the writer's imagination, but on a night like this with the rain and dark isolating him from the rest of the world, it was easy to let thoughts of things going bump in the night creep into your head. *If I had a laptop, or even a pad and a pen I'd write some of this stuff down and use it for a story.*

To fight off the boredom, Pierce used his optional hunting knife to make a wooden spoon out of one of the branches he had gathered for firewood. It wouldn't be fancy, but it would be better than trying to drink everything out of the pot or eating with his fingers. It also occupied an hour of his time.

When he was done with the spoon, he left the shelter of the tarp and climbed into his sleeping bag under the rock overhang. Since the camera gear was safely stored under the overhang with him, he had used the ten-foot by ten-foot tarp to cover his sleeping bag and the gear. It would keep him dry regardless of the rain and damp.

Pierce lay in the dark watching the fire burn down to glowing embers. As tired as he was from the day's work, thoughts of Katie, of things creeping unseen through the rain, and rumblings from his stomach kept him awake until well past midnight.

DAY 4

Peck woke to the sound of birds in the early morning. The rain had stopped and the sky, what he could see of it, was a vivid blue with no sign of any lingering clouds. Outside the tent the ground and surrounding woods were still wet so he elected to stay inside where it was warm and dry. It was the need to pee and to see the world outside the tent that finally drove him out.

He laughed to himself as he carried the table and propane stove outside to cook his breakfast. All he had to do to get it was open the cooler, take out a couple of eggs and cook them. They would go well with the leftover beans from the previous night. Chambers, on the other hand, was going to have to scrounge whatever he could from the wild. With any luck, the bastard would be cold, miserable and have to go hungry.

After he finished eating he realized there were several things he was going to need that he hadn't thought to bring. Enough water for washing as well as drinking, extra batteries for his lantern and extra propane for the stove, towels, and snack food. He was a snack food junkie. He'd make a list and then get them, and anything else he thought of, on the day he went back to town.

After an hour of sitting with no one to talk to and nothing to do but read, he decided to make his way over to Chambers' camp. He had intended to wait until dark, but the need to see how the prick was doing drew him like iron shavings to a magnet … or bears to honey. He hadn't gone more than a hundred yards before he turned back. The trail was still wet from the rain and the ground was slippery. *Screw this*, he thought after the ATV skidded and almost went off the road. *I'll wait until things dry out. Fucking with Chambers isn't worth getting injured.*

His decision to wait until the forest dried out lasted about an hour. Then the need to see how Chambers was coping drove him back into the woods.

Pierce didn't awake until several hours after sunrise. The overhang faced west and the surrounding forest kept the space well shaded. That, and the fact that he was awake well past midnight allowed him to get some well needed rest.

His first thought after climbing out of the sleeping bag was, *I've got to find something to eat.* It would be his first thought most days. Katie would be his second.

As soon as he was dressed, he turned on the camera to begin filming his day. "I never realized how easily life can descend to the search for food when you can't just go to the fridge or cupboard for something to eat. Last night I went to sleep hungry and this morning I woke up hungrier … and this is only Day 4. It's distressing to think there are people in the world who struggle with this every day.

"Fish would probably be the easiest, but I want some variety if I can get it. I also need some carbs and, hopefully, a little fruit. Maybe I can find some blueberries if I'm lucky.

"I'm not going to find blueberries in the woods, though, so I'm going to head back to the open area near the marsh." He picked up his bow and arrows and his pot and headed there, hoping to find some along the roads edge.

When he arrived at the road he noticed something he had overlooked on his previous visit—Asiatic dayflowers. He could use them as greens, either raw or lightly cooked. He marked the spot in his mind so he could gather them just before going back to camp. Then he found a real treasure, hopniss, also known as groundnut. The beautiful little purple flowers are what attracted his attention. He and Katie had eaten them on their first camping trip. They had been okay then, but now his mouth actually watered thinking about them.

"Look at this. See these flowers? That's groundnut. I can eat the tubers. I just have to dig them up. I'm not about to use my knife, though. I need to make a digging stick."

After he had fashioned one from the branch of a dead tree, he poked around with it until he found a tuber. Then he followed its rhizome to others. He filmed the entire process, all the while explaining what he was doing. When he had enough for the day's meal with some left over for the next day, he gathered some greens and then went back to the marsh in search of meat. Anything would do … frogs, snakes, crawfish, or anything else he could kill with the bow.

After thirty minutes of slogging through reeds and mud all he had to show for his efforts was one bullfrog. Two frog legs would have to do unless he wanted to eat some of the beef jerky from his emergency rations. Like the day before, when he came back to the camera, he thought he saw movement in the distance on the old road. And, like the last time, it was only there for an instant, and then it was gone. For a minute, Pierce had the uneasy feeling that someone, or something, was watching him. *Hey, maybe it's the little brothers*, he thought, and then laughed at himself.

On his way back to his shelter, Pierce found a mushroom that he recognized growing on the stump of a rotting oak tree. He trained the camera on it. "This is a 'chicken of the woods.' The field guide I bought rated it 'choice' for eating. It's unique, so I know that's what it is. I even watched a video of how to cook it on YouTube. I don't have garlic or oil, but I can cook it up in a stew with the hopniss, the dayflowers and the frog legs." Feeding himself was turning out to be easier than he had thought it would be. He just hoped it would last.

Once he had cleaned the frog and gathered water from the lake, Pierce went about starting a fire and cooking his "stew," filming it all and explaining what he was doing. He waited until the water was boiling before he threw in the hopniss. After letting the tubers cook until they were soft, like a boiled potato, he added the frog legs. When they looked done he dropped chopped dayflower greens into the mixture and immediately removed it from the fire. The greens would cook as the stew cooled enough to eat.

"Now, let's see how this tastes," he said as he dipped his new wooden spoon to the pot.

"Wow! I think I just became a big fan of hopniss," he told the camera after taking a bite of the tuber. "This broth is pretty good too," he added as he slurped the liquid from the wooden spoon. "I'm just going to let it cool off a little before I have any more."

As he sat back to wait for the soup to cool, grunting noises came from the ridge above the overhang. "Did you hear that?" he asked the camera. Then he fell silent, listening to see if the noise would come again. A minute later, it did … along with the sounds of something moving through the underbrush.

"I think that's a bear. I heard it the other night, too. As long as it stays up there and I'm down here, I'm okay with it. Just in case though, I'm going to make a little noise. It's supposed to scare them off, so here goes," he told the camera.

"Nothing down here for you bear, just little old me," he called into the night. "You can go back to wherever it is you go when you're not here." Then he listened again to see if it was still moving around. The sounds didn't come again.

"Tomorrow I'm going to take a look and see what's there," he told the camera before turning it off.

It was still an hour until sunset when he finished eating, so he decided to go exploring. The moon was moving toward full, but he still wanted to be back before the sun set. But right now, he couldn't just sit here staring at the fire waiting for the night. If he did, thoughts of Katie would overwhelm him.

Before he left he put enough wood on the fire to keep it going until he returned. He took the bow with him just in case he had an opportunity to score a meal.

Pierce walked to the lake and started to make his way around it. At some places the trees ran right up to the bank. At others, they stopped a few feet from the edge. At one place there was an open area that abutted a shallow spot where he could easily get in and out to bathe. He'd do that tomorrow when he could lie on a sunbaked rock to dry off.

He got back to his camp before the sun dropped below the horizon. As the dark closed in around him, loneliness once again gripped him. "This being alone is hard," he told the camera. "For as long as I can remember I've never been more than inches away from a cell phone or computer." Social media had become as much a part of his life as actual face-to-face contact with friends. Hell, he actually had more friends and followers on social media than in real life.

"I'd sleep all night if I could, just so I don't have to be alone in the dark. The daytime isn't so bad. I can hunt for food, explore the woods, and gather firewood. Tomorrow I'll go swimming and wash some clothes. All I can do at night is sit and watch this fire. That's when my mind runs wild. I listen for sounds in the woods and when I hear them I wonder what they are. Is it a bear? Then I think about Katie, or Hautala's little brothers. I know they're not real, but they scare the hell out of me anyway." (They didn't, really, but it would make for good video.)

Just as he finished talking, a weird, undulating call broke the silence. "For those of you who never heard one of those, that was a loon. I think I was twelve the first time I heard one and it scared the hell out of me. I thought it was a ghost." A few minutes later, it came again. "Eerie, but beautiful, isn't it?

"That's it. I'm going to shut things down for the day. It's early, but I'm going to try to get some sleep."

When he climbed into his sleeping bag, Pierce knew he would lie awake and think of Katie. She was a blessing and a curse. She dominated his thoughts, which both thrilled him and ate at him. More than anything else, he wanted to be home with her.

Just as he was falling asleep, the howling of a coyote split the quiet of the night. He sat up, all thoughts of sleep forgotten. *Coyote. Nothing to really worry about, but I'll put some more wood on the fire just to be sure.*

As he was feeding the first log to the flames, the yipping came again. He wasn't sure, but he thought it came from the same place the bear's grunts had come from. *I'm definitely going to check that out. I don't want to move my camp, but I will if I have to.*

When Peck arrived at the logging road he scanned the marsh with his binoculars. He saw the camera set up on its tripod, but Chambers was nowhere in sight. He considered staying where he was, but wanted to get a bit closer for a better look at what he was doing. He hadn't taken two steps when the prick came out of the reeds, bow in hand. "Shit," he swore and jumped back into the bushes at the side of the road. He doubted Chambers had seen him, but he kept down just in case. When he finally risked looking up, Chambers was gone.

That was close. I'll wait till tonight, he thought, and headed back to his tent.

Peck popped a beer and put a steak on the grill portion of the stove. *I don't know what Chambers is eating for dinner, but I'm sure it's not anything like this.* Two ears of corn on the cob were already steaming in the pot on the side burner.

After dinner he sat outside the tent reading until sunset. Then he moved inside. At ten o'clock by his watch, he donned his night goggles, climbed on the ATV, and made his way toward Chambers.

The ride and walk over was easier that it had been two days ago. The growing moon provided more light and now he knew the way. Still, he had to be careful.

It was midnight when he reached the spot above Chambers, he played the recording of the coyote. It gave him chills, and *he* knew it was just a recording. *Hah, you heard that, didn't you?* he thought when the light coming from the prick's fire flared and glowing sparks rose into the sky. Peck grinned to himself. Chambers must have put another log on the fire. Satisfied, Peck made his way back to his tent.

DAY 5

Pierce woke hungry, but he was getting used to that. His first thought was to go fishing, but he changed his mind. Instead, he set up the camera and talked to it.

"It's day five, and, as usual, I'm hungry as hell. I could go fishing, but I want to check out the area where I think I heard the coyote and the bear. So, for now, I think I'm going to have a piece or two of the beef jerky I brought along just to take the edge off. Then I'm going to see what's up there. You wanna come?"

Pierce kept the camera running as he made his way along the rock ledge looking for an easy way up. He didn't want to risk climbing it and falling. He wasn't willing to take that risk out here. Eventually he found where the ledge dwindled away into the ground. Then he reversed direction, following the ridgeline back toward his camp.

He stayed a few feet back from the edge as the escarpment rose, cautious not to slip on the dead leaves, or trip on the tree roots hidden in them and tumble off the ledge. A wisp of smoke from his fire told him when he had arrived at the spot above his camp. He carefully made his way to the edge and panned the camera over the top of his shelter and the surrounding area.

"That's it. That's my camp. It doesn't look like much from here, but it's home. Now let's take a look around and see if I can find anything."

He kept filming as he searched the area for any signs of the bear or coyote he had heard in the night. "Look here, the ground has been disturbed, but I don't see any tracks or scat. Wait a minute, look at this," he said, and zoomed in the bit of hair Peck had left for him to find. "Could that be from a bear?" he asked as he plucked it from a broken branch. "But if a bear was here, there should be tracks—something more than this. I don't get it."

Pierce turned the camera off and continued to search the area. He found signs that something had passed through the woods. They led back toward the old logging road. Instead of following them, he retraced his steps and headed back to his camp intent on finding something to eat. Along the way, he found another chicken of the forest.

When he reached his camp, he dropped off the mushroom, grabbed his fishing line and headed to the lake. Along the way he searched for bait among the dead leaves and fallen trees. "God, I hope I never have to eat these things," he said, holding the grubs he found out for the camera to see. "I don't care what Bear Grylls says, I'll pass. I'm just happy the fish love them. Before I use them, though, I'm going to take a swim."

When he got to the place he had found the day before, Pierce set up the camera, stood in front of it, and started to strip off his clothes. When he got down to his briefs he waggled his finger and said, "Okay, that's enough skin. I'll see you when I'm done."

Once he had doffed his briefs, he stepped into the lake. He had expected it to be freezing, but it wasn't; it was actually quite pleasant.

After swimming for ten minutes he made his way back to the shallows. Just before climbing out, he noticed a fresh-water mussel nestled among the weeds on the bottom. *Yes*, he thought as he reached down and picked it up.

Back on shore, he turned the camera on and held the mussel out for his audience. "This is a fresh-water mussel and they're edible. I'm going to see how many of them I can find. Maybe I won't have to fish today after all."

Returning to the water, he had no trouble collecting two dozen mussels … more than enough for a meal. Before dressing, he dumped the grubs out, placed the mussels into the pot and filled it with water.

When he returned to camp, he steamed the mussels and then boiled them along with the mushroom, filming the entire thing.

"Well, that's it. I've gone swimming, found a bunch of mussels, eaten my lunch, and I still have at least five hours of daylight left. I can either sit and brood, or get out and do something. I think I'll go exploring. So, what do you say we take a walk and see what we can find? Hopefully, it'll be something good."

Instead of heading left back to the logging road, he went in the opposite direction, keeping the water on his left. After two hours of walking he hadn't found anything of interest other than a stream that fed into the lake. Disappointed, he made his way back to his camp to make a fire before the sun went down.

What the hell happed here? Pierce thought as he approached his shelter. Things were scattered all around the campsite.

Shit, I wonder if anything's missing? A quick look around assured him nothing was, but it made him suspicious. *What the hell? A bear would have torn everything apart. A person would have taken something. But nothing's ruined and nothing's been taken. Somebody's fucking with me.*

Pierce filmed the wreckage as he put his camp back in shape. "This is what I found when I came back today. I thought it might be a bear, or some other animal, but nothing was ripped or torn apart. Then I thought someone might have found my camp, but nothing's missing. It could be a kid, but what would a kid be doing way out here? No, I think somebody's messing with me." He didn't say it, but Peck was at the top of his list of suspects.

Even though he had access to books and music on his iPad that Chambers didn't, Peck was experiencing some of the same feelings of isolation that Chambers was. Sitting all day waiting for night was eating on him.

I need to do something. I can't just sit around here all day. It's driving me crazy. Playing sounds in the dark isn't enough. I need to ramp things up. I'm going over to Chambers' camp. If he sees me I'll just tell him I'm checking on him to make sure he's following the rules. He'd believe that. I'll to go back to the ridge overlooking his campsite get a look at what he's doing.

As he approached the site he listened for any hint that Chambers might be there. When he didn't hear anything, he moved closer until he reached the spot above his camp where he had been in the night. It was obvious Chambers had already been there. The leaf litter on the ground had been scuffed around and the bit of bear hair he had left was missing. *Good, I've got his attention.*

He was about to leave when he heard Chambers coming from the woods to his right. He knew he couldn't be seen from where he was, but he still dropped to the ground. It wasn't long before he heard the asshole talking to the camera about steaming some mussels and making a soup out of them and a mushroom.

Son of a bitch, he's got mussels and mushrooms. I hope he gets a bad one. And where the hell did he get mussels from? I thought they only lived in salt water.

As he lay on his stomach listening to Chambers narrate his dinner, Peck debated whether he should leave or stay. The decision was made for him when Chambers declared, "So, what do you say we take a walk and see what we can find? Hopefully, it'll be something good."

Great, get the fuck out of here. I want to check out your camp, Peck thought as he waited for Chambers to leave.

When he was sure he was gone, Peck hustled to the end of the escarpment and then to the camp. He was surprised and pissed at what he found. The prick had actually made himself a decent place to live. The large tarp covered his fire pit, and logs had been arranged to form a seat and a table. *Where the hell is he sleeping?* he thought as he rifled through Chambers' gear. Then he discovered the overhang. This pissed him off even more. It was as if nature had provided him with the perfect bedroom.

Well, fuck you, Chambers, he thought, and trashed the camp. He scattered the firewood, pissed in the fire pit, and tossed the rest of the gear around. *Let's see how you like that, Asshole.*

DAY 5 – NIGHT

Pierce stared up at the night sky through the swirling smoke from his fire. He could just make out the moon through an opening in the foliage. The night wasn't quite as dark as it had been on his first night, but the moon still didn't cast enough light for him to be comfortable venturing away from his fire. He didn't need a broken arm or ankle from wandering around in the dark. Nonetheless, he was glad to see it and he told the camera so. "The moon's getting brighter. When it's full I'm going to do some bass fishing with a frog as bait. I used to bass fish with my dad at night when I was a kid. We used a Hula Popper then, sort of an artificial frog. But a real, live frog should be even better."

He was getting ready to turn the camera off when a loud grunting noise came from above him. It didn't sound like the bear from the other night but it could be. Then there was a lot of thrashing and the sound of breaking branches. "What the hell? Something's up there" he whispered into the camera. Then a shower of dead leaves fell off the ridge and onto his tarp. "Damn," he swore and scrambled for his air horn and wild animal repellent. "That has to be an animal. No one would be out here in the dark this time of night." He was ready to set off the air horn when he heard whatever it was crashing away through the night. "Listen, I think it's going away."

Once whatever it was gone, silence fell over the forest. Not silence, exactly, the normal sounds of the night were still there … wind in the trees, the distant call of a loon and the crackling of his fire, but there were no more grunts or cracking branches. Still, he sat next to the fire with the air horn and animal repellent close at hand.

"It's going to be a long night," he told the camera as he stuck a branch in the fire and left the other end sticking out so he could grab it and use it as a flaming club if he needed it.

As the night wore on and there was no reoccurrence of the disturbance on the ridge, Pierce found himself nodding off in spite of himself. When he almost fell off his log he gave up trying to stay awake.

"That's it, I'm going to bed."

Before retreating to his sleeping bag with the air horn and animal repellent, he built the fire up so it would last as long as possible. He doubted he'd be able to sleep, but was gone as soon as his head hit his makeshift pillow.

Pierce heard grunts and snapping branches and this time they weren't coming from the ridge above him. They were coming from the trees just beyond the light thrown from his fire. At first he saw nothing. Then a pair of glowing red eyes appeared in the night. They were soon followed by a dozen more. He lay frozen in his sleeping bag, afraid to move or make a sound.

What the hell are they? Then a small, humanoid creature stepped into the light thrown by the fire.

Little brothers! They're real! The thought burned through his mind and broke his paralysis. He reached for the air horn and animal repellent, but they were gone. He reached for his bow. He only had six arrows, but if he could kill just one of them, maybe the others would turn tail back into the dark.

More of the creatures came into the firelight as he hurried to string the bow. He almost had it when the bow string snapped. All he had left now was his knife. The axe was under the tarp near the fire.

The lead creature must have heard the snap of the bow string because it turned its gaze in Pierce's direction. When it saw him, its mouth opened in a fierce grin filled with sharp, glittering teeth. Then it screamed, and the entire tribe rushed him.

He woke, struggling to get out of his sleeping bag just before the pack was about to reach him.

Peck started out for Chambers' camp as soon as the sun started to set, knowing that by the time he reached it, it would be full dark. The night-vision goggles gobbled the light the moon provided and made it easy for him make his way through the woods.

When he reached the point above Chambers, he played the grunting and growling noises on his iPad. Then he started thrashing around in the undergrowth, snapping branches and growling. He used a branch to push leaves and twigs over the edge, knowing they would shower down on the asshole's camp. He kept the act up for five minutes before breaking it off and heading toward the logging road. He was back in his tent before Pierce crawled into his sleeping bag.

DAY 6

When his heart finally stopped trying to rip itself out of his chest, Pierce realized it was just a dream. The eyes in the dark, the little brothers—all just a dream, a really bad dream. He felt a surge of relief until he peered into the woods. They were lost in a deep, gray fog. Still reeling from the dream, he thought he saw shapes moving among the trees.

Just my imagination. There's nothing out there. But, as he lay wrapped in his sleeping bag, he couldn't get the little brothers out of his head.

Get up, you idiot. Start a fire, do something, anything.

"Hey! Getting up here," he called, hoping to scare away anything that might be out there. He strained to hear anything moving in the gray veil beyond his tarp, but there was just unbroken silence. When the plaintive cry of a loon broke the stillness he nearly pissed himself.

I need to film this, he thought, remembering the camera.

"Look what I woke up to this morning … fog. It's creepy as hell. There could be anything out there … a bear, deer, moose, coyote, and I wouldn't know it. It's scary and cool, all at the same time. It's so damp I hope I'm going to be able to get a fire started."

Pierce aimed the camera at the fire where a thin tendril of smoke rose toward the top of the tarp.

"Hey, maybe I'm in luck. It looks like there are still some coals burning in there. Let's see." When he stirred the ashes he revealed a bed of glowing embers under a layer of ash the same color as the fog. "Yes! Let's get this fire going and get the chill out."

Once the fire was established, Pierce put the pot of water he had gotten the night before on the fire to boil. "I'm going to dip into my rice and jerky today. It's too damn damp and nasty to be wandering around in the woods if I don't have to. As a matter of fact, I think I'm going to climb back into my sleeping bag after I eat. It's warm and dry in there."

It was warm and dry, but it was also a mind trap. With nothing to keep him occupied, his thoughts turned to Katie. *God, I miss her. I wish I could dream of her instead of the little brothers.*

He was snapped out of his thoughts of Katie by something moving in the gray curtain surrounding him. He was sure of it. As he listened, the panic of the dream gripped him. *I've got to get out of this sleeping bag. I'm trapped in here if something attacks me.*

He slipped out of the bag as quietly as he could. Then he strung is bow and waited for whatever it was to appear out of the fog. When he looked at his hands they were shaking. *Get ahold of yourself, Chambers. You couldn't hit a school bus right now.*

The fog thinned as he waited. Soon he could almost make out the trees. They were just lumbering shapes without definition, but he was relieved to see them just the same. Then two squirrels bounded out of the mist, racing through the dead leaves on the forest floor. Pierce actually laughed at himself. Here were the noise makers that had seemed so threatening. At the sound of his voice, both squirrels retreated back into the fog and Pierce could hear them scampering up a tree.

As more trees materialized out of the fog, he yielded to the need to get out of the confines of his shelter. This time he took the bow and arrows along as well as the camera.

Pierce nocked an arrow as he approached the spot above his camp where the activity had taken place the night before. The last time he had visited the spot he had to look carefully to find the signs that something had been there. Not now. Several branches were broken and the forest floor was a mess. There were deep claw marks in the dirt where the dead leaves had been tossed around. No squirrel did this. "Damn," he swore, looking around nervously. "If it comes back again I'm finding another campsite."

Pierce detoured to the marsh on his way back to the campsite.

"Might as well try and find something to eat," he said out loud. He didn't know when the habit had started, but he was talking to himself now just to hear a voice, even if it was his own.

Reaching the marsh, he crept around the edge as quietly as he could. The going was easier because his previous trips had beaten down much of the grass and underbrush, making something of a path. He was about to take a shot at a large bullfrog when a movement in the reeds ten feet from shore caught his eye. He froze in place waiting to see what it was. A minute later, a male mallard came picking its way toward him, its emerald green head shining in the sun.

Do I shoot it? It's not hunting season, but damn, I sure could use it. In the end his need for meat won the argument.

The duck seemed to be completely unaware as Pierce raised the bow and drew the arrow back to his cheek. *If I miss, I'll probably lose this arrow, but I've got five more so it's worth it.*

He took careful aim and let the arrow fly. It hit the mallard square in the breast, but didn't kill it. The bird flapped and struggled with the arrow sticking out of its breast.

"Damn, I hit it, but now I have to go get it. I can't do it like this. There's no way I'm going in there wearing my shoes and pants. I'm going to have to strip down to my shorts."

Yuck, he thought as his feet sank into several inches of mud. He felt it squeeze between his toes, slippery and cold. Bubbles broke the surface releasing noxious fumes that smelled like rotting garbage and he almost gagged. He was tempted to turn back and leave the duck. If the thing hadn't been flopping around and suffering he might have, so he pushed on. When he finally reached the bird, he grabbed it and snapped its neck before turning around and making his way back to shore.

"What the hell?" he exclaimed when he bent to reach for his pants. His legs were covered in leeches from the knees down. There were at five on his right leg and four on the left. And those were only the ones he could see. The first one twisted away from him when he grabbed it with his fingers to pull it off. It slipped out of his grasp and stayed firmly planted on his leg. Steeling himself, he used his thumb and middle finger to pinch it at the point it was attached to his skin. Blood squirted out of it when he finally managed to yank it off. It left a tiny, bleeding hole where it had been attached.

He fought the urge not to vomit and worked on plucking the rest off. Before he did, though, he set the camera up to film it. "I got these hunting for frogs," he lied as he zoomed in for a close-up on one of the leeches. "Watch what happens when I pull it off." Then he stepped far enough back to allow the camera to film him removing the rest.

When he had finished, he had plucked eleven of them from his legs.

"I've got to wash these. I can't afford to let them get infected," he said before he turned the camera off.

As soon as he got back to his shelter, he grabbed his pot and made his way to the lake where he stripped naked and walked into the water. This time the chill of it gave him goose flesh and helped stop any more bleeding from his wounds. He washed them as best he could, rubbing his hands over them to remove any dirt and slime from the marsh.

"This is not as easy as they make it look on television," he complained as he tried to pluck the feathers from the mallard. "I've killed this thing, so I'm not going to throw it way. I'm going to pluck it, clean it, cook it and eat it."

An hour later, he was roasting it over the fire, amazed at how much grease dripped from the bird into the flames. It wasn't until he was eating, that he realized he could have saved the fat and used it for cooking. He had a lot to learn about this survival stuff.

Pierce had just turned the camera off when he realized he had to delete everything concerning the duck. *Crap, if this stuff ever hits YouTube, I could be in a world of trouble for killing a duck out of season. Peck would make sure of that. I'm going to have to delete most of it. Too bad, it's good video and something different. I'll leave the leeches, though. That's the kind of shit people like.*

Even though the fog had completely burned off, the day was still overcast and the threat of rain hung in the air as evening approached. "It's going to rain. I can feel it. I need to get out of here for a while before it does. I can't stand the thought of being trapped here again with nothing to do. It's driving me crazy," he told the camera. "I'm going to look for an alternative campsite." Pierce followed the outcropping, talking to the camera, which was strapped to his chest, as he went. From time to time the bow and arrows he was carrying in his left hand would pass through the camera's view as he walked. Every time he heard a noise he would flinch. The further he got away from his camp site, the more nervous he became. It was probably irrational, but he felt safer there. Here, in the woods, he felt too exposed.

"I'm going back. I want to beat any rain," he said within fifteen minutes of leaving what he now considered home. The quaver in his voice showed how nervous he was. The fog, the leeches and the solitude were weighing heavily on his mood.

Back at the camp, he huddled under the tarp and waited for nightfall. The rain started as a light drizzle before turning into a steady, soaking rain that kept him huddled under the tarp waiting to see what new noises the night would bring.

"Fucking rain," Peck mumbled as he sat in his tent looking out through the open fly. *Pierce must be going bugshit crazy over there. I can hardly stand it myself. Thank God I've got a day off tomorrow. Stanley can sit out here for a while.*

As he peered through the partially open door of the tent, he saw something move between the trees in the distance. He stared, trying to see what it was. It was big and dark but obscured by the rain and gloom of the overcast shadows. *What the hell is that?*

He watched it for several minutes, hardly daring to blink or breathe. When it failed to move again, he convinced himself it was just a shadow against the background of the woods, and that he had imagined the movement. He finally let out a sigh of relief and poured himself another cup of coffee. When he looked back up, the shadow was gone.

Get a grip. A trick of the light, that's all it was, he thought as he sipped his coffee. *Wait, there it is again, in the same spot. I'm sure of it. What the hell is it?*

This time as he watched, the shadow slowly melted into the background. It didn't move … it just faded away. Bare trees now stood where it had been. *A trick of the light … it has to be.*

He continued to watch as the forest darkened with the coming night. Soon the spot where he had seen the movement was lost to the deepening gloom. Eventually he turned on his lantern and closed the tent's fly. Then he lit the propane stove to drive the damp away.

From outside, the light from the lantern created silhouettes on the tent's walls. Once again, Peck was putting on a show for the watchers in the woods.

DAY 7

The rain had stopped, but fog once again enveloped the woods when Pierce rolled out of his sleeping bag. "I can't sit here another day," he told the camera. "I'll go crazy if I do. I need to find something to eat. I think it's going to be fish … again. I've never eaten so much fish in my life. It's a good thing I like perch."

Water dripped from the trees as he made his way to the rotten tree where he had been gathering grubs. "Damn," he swore when he saw it. The tree had been torn apart, with pieces of it scattered around like tissue paper on Christmas morning. "This had to be a bear. Nothing else could have done this."

Suddenly the fog became a lot scarier than it had been. Everything he had heard about bears said to make a lot of noise so they would know you were there, but the last thing he wanted to do was to draw attention to himself. What he wanted even less was to walk up on it by accident. Frozen by indecision, he sat down and stayed where he was, waiting for the fog to lift.

The plaintive cry of a loon and the rapid "knock- knock-knock" of a woodpecker echoed through the fog before Pierce heard a soft grunting coming from somewhere in front of him. *Jesus*, he thought and tried to make himself smaller.

As the sounds came closer, a figure started to emerge from the mist. It was a black bear, a big one. When Pierce gasped, it lifted its head and looked at him. They stared at each other for several minutes, neither moving, before it turned and faded back into the fog. He was so shaken by the experience that by the time he remembered the camera strapped to his chest it was too late, the bear was gone.

Holy shit! That was scary. What a rush! Damn, I should have got that on tape. But then again, who knows what it would have done it I had tried. Maybe it would have taken that as a threat. But still, it would have been amazing. I can tell people about it, but would they believe it without seeing it? Probably not if Peck has anything to say about it. He'd say I made it all up. What the hell, let him. I know it happened.

It was too late to get the bear on camera, but he turned it on anyway and panned it across the fog-filled woods. "I just saw a bear. It spooked me so bad I was ready to tap out. But it didn't bother me. It knew I was here and it left me alone. I think that as long as I leave it alone, it'll leave me alone. This might sound stupid, but I'm willing to give it a try. I might even be able to get it on camera. Besides, if I tap out just because I saw a bear, I'll look like a real pussy. I couldn't do that to everyone who is rooting for me."

Despite the bravado for the camera, he sat unmoving for a full hour waiting for the fog to completely burn off before he felt safe enough to move.

The next time he turned the camera on he was pointing it at a small frog. "See that? I'm hoping that's dinner. No, I'm not going to eat it … I'm going to use it as bait if I can catch it."

He left the camera running on its tripod as he tried to sneak up on the frog. He was just ready to reach out and grab it when it launched itself into the water and disappeared. Feeling a bit foolish, he turned and grinned back at the camera. "Well that sucks, but I'm not giving up. I'm going to catch at least one of the little buggers even if it takes all day. And if I don't … at least you guys will get a good laugh out of it."

By the time Pierce returned to the camera he looked like the loser in a mud wrestling contest. That didn't stop him from proudly holding up a squirming frog for his future audience to see. "Here it is," he bragged, "food for Mister Bass. I just hope he's hungry, because I sure am."

The next time the camera was on, Pierce was hooking the frog through its mouth with a number 1/0 barbed hook. "I'm going to toss this guy out there and let him swim around. Hopefully he'll attract the attention of a bass." After saying that he tossed the frog into the lake, allowing the line to unwrap off its spool. It only went about fifteen feet, but he hoped it would be enough.

Pierce watched the frog flounder around on the surface waiting for a bass to hit. When nothing happened he brought it back in and moved further down the bank. After trying for an hour, the frog was dead. "No luck," he told the camera as he removed it from the hook and tossed it in the lake. Its white belly shone like a ghost as it sank into the depths. Then, suddenly, a dark shape materialized from nowhere, sucked it into its mouth, and quickly disappeared.

"Son of a bitch. There goes my dinner." Then he started laughing. "All that and the damn thing outsmarted me. You win today, fish, but now I know where you are. I'll be back for you tomorrow."

Pierce didn't have go hungry, he knew that, but the camera didn't need to know it. He had plenty of rice and jerky. He had only been here seven days but hunger had already become his constant companion. Every contestant talked about it on all the survival shows, but there was no way they could ever convey how pervasive it became. It was a constant gnaw in his stomach. Only seven days, and he knew he had already lost weight. His body was slowly eating itself.

Peck rolled out of bed about the same time as Chambers. Unlike Chambers, though, all he had to do to find his breakfast was open his cooler. Today he was having fried eggs, breakfast sausage, coffee and orange juice. The fog greeted him when he went outside to take a leak. *Fuck this*, he thought as he stood shivering while he relieved himself. As soon as he was done he retreated to the warmer, drier environment of the tent and went about cooking his breakfast and brewing coffee.

When he was done, he lay back down on his cot and read, knowing the alarm on his iPhone would tell him when it was time to climb onto the ATV and head to the drop-off point to meet Stanley.

The sun had burned the fog off by the time he had to leave. On the ride to the meeting place, Pierce filled his thoughts. *Well,*

Chambers, you get a break tonight, but I'll be back tomorrow. Then it's time for the good stuff.

Stanley was waiting at the gate when Peck arrived at twelve thirty. "I was starting to wonder if you were coming. You said to be here at noon."

"Yeah, well, I had to take it slow. There was a lot of fog this morning. Plus, I didn't want to dig up the path too much. I don't want to make it too obvious that we're out here. We don't want some nosey asshole to come poking around."

"Right," Stanley agreed, handing him the keys to the pickup.

After they unloaded the food, Stanley handed Peck the key to the motel room he had rented.

"All right. I'll meet you back here tomorrow at noon. Don't go near Chambers. I'll take care of that tomorrow."

"You got it," Stanley told him as he climbed aboard the ATV.

Peck waited until Stanley was out of sight before climbing into the pickup and heading into town. He was in the shower within minutes of dumping his stuff on the second bed in the motel room Stanley had rented for them. When he was done and dressed, he took out his laptop and posted some more Bigfoot pics.

Whoa, look at this guy! Like I said, Chambers is camping in Bigfoot country. There have been documented Bigfoot sightings in the same area for hundreds of years. I was skeptical at first, but the museum here has all sorts of pictures and articles from locals who claim to have seen the creature. I've got to wonder if Chambers has run into one yet. We won't know until he comes back. If he comes back, that is.

Katie was furious when she saw the post with the picture of Peck standing next to the lifelike Bigfoot. The asshole hadn't posted since the day she had dropped Pierce off, and now she knew why. He was up there, and whatever he was doing couldn't be good. She wanted to fire off a snarky comment, but didn't want Peck to realize who she was and unfriend her. She had sent him a friend request shortly after Pierce had told her about him and he had accepted right away. Luckily, her profile picture was a copy of Van Gogh's *Starry Night*, so he didn't recognize her when they met. She wanted to keep it that way.

Tomorrow I'm going up there. I'm going to see what that asshole is up to. But right now, I have to get to work.

If knowing Pierce was on his own in the Maine woods wasn't bad enough, knowing that Peck was there too only made it worse. She was on edge her entire shift and only picked at her dinner once she got home.

"What's wrong? Worried about Pierce?" her mother asked.

Katie told her about Peck's post and her worries that he was doing something to interfere with Pierce.

"Well, there's nothing you can do about it. Is there?"

"I don't know, but I'm going to drive up there and see what's going on."

DAY 8

For Pierce, Day 8 started out like every other day—he woke up hungry. "I wonder how much weight I've lost?" he asked as he cinched his belt in front of the camera. "I've already dropped a notch. I'm glad Katie fattened me up before I came out here."

Pierce held one of his shirts up in front of the camera. "I'm going to dig up some more groundnut and then I'm going to catch a few bullfrogs. This time, though, I'm going to use a fish-hook and a piece of red cloth from this shirt. I wish I would have thought of it sooner."

He continued to film as he used his knife cut a piece of cloth the size of a dime from the shirt. Then he tied the hook and five feet of line to a ten-foot sapling he had cut and stripped of branches. When he was done, he stepped back and dangled the hook in front of the camera. "When I see a frog, I'll dangle this in front of its nose and jiggle it up and down like a bug. It should snag it with its tongue and pull it back into its mouth. Then all I have to do then is set the hook. Presto, dinner."

The camera zoomed in on a bullfrog with just its head visible above the surface. Suddenly, the bit of red cloth entered the frame. It bounced and danced in front of the frog's nose. At first nothing happened. Then, almost too fast for the eye to follow, a long, white tongue darted out and snagged the bit of cloth. As soon as it disappeared into the frog's mouth, Pierce yanked on the line and lifted it out of the water.

The frog struggled as he swung it toward shore. It pawed at the line with its front legs, but the hook had pierced the bright yellow skin on the underside of its mouth. Once he had it safely in hand, Pierce held it in front of the camera before taking it off frame to kill it. He repeated the process until he had four good-sized frogs for his meal.

He didn't bother filming each frog as he cut the legs off. He did film the last one though. When he was done he held the leg-less body up for his audience to see. "This," he said, "is going into the lake. I'm not leaving it here to attract scavengers. Now, let's go get some of that groundnut."

On the way back to camp, Pierce kept an eye out for another chicken of the woods. He had developed a real taste for them. Unfortunately, there were none to be had. He did find several other mushrooms, but he wasn't sure if they were safe, so he passed them by. Then he found some he recognized. Or, at least he was pretty sure he did, so he grabbed a few and stuck them in the pot with the frog legs and the groundnut.

By the time he had a fire going, Pierce thought his stomach was going to jump out of his body and attack the food. He actually considered eating the frog legs raw. Instead, he ate a piece of jerky to take the edge off.

Once the water was boiling he dropped the groundnut and mushrooms in. Then he hung the legs over the flames to let them roast. "It won't be long now," he told the camera.

Pierce filmed the pot as the groundnuts and mushrooms cooked and the legs as they grilled. When they were done he took the pot off the fire to cool. While he waited for that, he devoured the frog legs.

Still famished, Pierce consumed the groundnut and mush-rooms in a matter of minutes. Then he drank the broth they had cooked in. "Man, that was good," he said, smiling at the camera. He didn't notice the tingling on his tongue until the pot was empty.

"What the hell?" he mumbled, sticking his fingers into his mouth and grabbing his tongue. It was numb. "Shit! Were those the wrong mushrooms? I've got to get rid of them." He stuck his fingers down his throat to try and make himself vomit. Bits of mushroom, frog legs and groundnut spewed from his mouth, but the damage was already done.

Slowly, the light coming through the trees grew brighter and broke apart into colors. Sounds that had been in the background assaulted him. The scurrying of a pair of squirrels sounded like an army coming toward him. A log shifted in the fire and sparks rose from the flames like a blazing phoenix. The world was going wild. A loon's haunting call sent him fleeing to the back of his rock shelter, shaking in fear.

Suddenly he became aware that something big was moving through the trees. He only caught glimpses of it as it darted from place to place, fading in and out of the shadows. When it finally stood still long enough for him to get a good look at it, he recoiled in fear. He was looking directly at Bigfoot. As he tried to crab even deeper into his cover, his hand brushed the bow. He wanted to string it and nock an arrow but he was so terrified he couldn't get his hands to work. Instead, he crammed his body up against the back of the overhang and cowered under his sleeping bag.

The effects of the mushroom didn't wear off until the sun started to peek through the trees. He found himself crouched under the rock overhang clutching his bow. He wasn't sure what he had seen in the night, but he wasn't willing to venture out from the overhang to start a fire.

Peck started his day at seven by rolling out of a comfy full-sized bed. He showered, packed his clean clothes into his suitcase and went to Polly's Café for a breakfast of pancakes, sausage, OJ and coffee. He ate in leisure, reading a copy of the local paper. When he was done, he drove out to the meeting place to meet Stanley. He couldn't wait to get back to the tent. He had big plans for Chambers today.

"How was your night in town?" Stanley asked when he arrived on the ATV.

"Fine. I'll see you at noon in three days. Help me load this stuff up," Peck answered and flipped him the keys to the pickup.

Five minutes later he was on his way back to the tent. His clean clothes and a cooler full of food and beer along with a second cooler packed with ice were on the trailer behind him. They were all were strapped down with bungie cords so they wouldn't bounce around too much.

The ride back took forever. He thought about the next phase

of his plan the entire way. When he finally arrived, he hastily unloaded the groceries. As soon as they were put away, he stripped down to his underwear and got into his costume. It had cost him seventy bucks on the internet and would never pass a close inspection, but it would do. It might not be seven feet tall like the one in the museum, but from a distance it wouldn't matter.

"Shit, there's no way I can drive in this thing," he swore when he tried to drive the ATV with the costume on. He took off the head and tried that, but he still couldn't manage. Eventually, he had to take the entire thing off and drive in his underwear, but he was okay with that. He didn't want to take the time to go back in the tent and put the rest of his clothes on.

He stopped the ATV while he was still a mile from the marsh. *This is close enough. I don't want him to hear me coming.* He thought about leaving the costume off until he got closer but decided against it. Sure as hell if he did, he'd run into Chambers and that would ruin everything. Once he donned the Bigfoot outfit his field of vision was limited with the headpiece on. After falling twice, he removed it and carried it under one arm. Wearing it at home and in the tent hadn't been a problem, but out here it the woods it was clumsy as hell. He'd put it back on when he got closer.

He smelled the smoke from Chambers' fire before he actually saw the camp. There was still an hour of daylight left, enough for Chambers to spot him through the trees. He put the headpiece on and was ready to let Chambers see him when he remembered the bow. *I'd better not get too close, I don't want that asshole to shoot me.*

As soon as the headpiece was in place, his vision was reduced to what was directly in front of him. He carefully picked his way through the woods until he saw the flicker of flames through the trees. Chambers!

He crept closer to get a good look at the prick's camp. The fire was blazing, but Chambers was nowhere in sight. *Where the hell is he?* Then he saw him, huddled under the rock ledge behind the tarp. It looked like he was hiding back there. Peck made a few grunting noises to draw his attention. He was prepared to retreat back into the woods if Chambers grabbed the bow and arrows.

Chambers' head snapped up when Peck made some chuffing noises. When he failed to react any further, Peck shuffled between two trees. This time he was sure Chambers saw him because the prick scuttled further back under his rock.

What's the matter, Adventure Boy, scared? Did you just piss yourself?

Peck moved from place to place, always staying in Chambers' line of sight but never getting close enough to give him a good look. He was ready to retreat into the woods if Chambers left his rock shelter, but he never did. After ten minutes, Peck faded back into the woods to return to his own camp. Even if he had been paying attention, he wouldn't have heard the footsteps following him. Their owner was too stealthy, too used to moving through the woods unseen and unheard.

Katie was out of bed, showered, dressed, and on the road by seven. "Aren't you going to eat something?" her mother called to her as she hurried through the kitchen without stopping.

"I want to get going. I'll grab something on the way." What she grabbed was a ham, egg and cheese croissant sandwich, coffee, and an orange juice from the drive thru at Burger King. She had to pass two McDonald's to reach it, but after working at Mickey D's for a year right after high school, she had vowed never to eat at one again. She knew Burger King probably wasn't much better, but it didn't matter. She couldn't bring herself eat at the clown's place.

She still had the coordinates on her phone's GPS so she let it lead her to the General Store. From there she knew the way to the old logging road. She had no idea what she was going to find or do once she got there. She only knew that she felt better with every mile she got closer to where Pierce was.

When she passed the motel they had stayed in on the drive up, any good feelings Katie had evaporated. She slowed to a stop and turned around before it had disappeared from sight in her review mirror. When she got back to it, she pulled into the parking lot and broke down in tears. Once she pulled herself together, she got back on the road, more determined than ever to find out what Peck was up to.

When she reached it, the drop-off was empty. She hadn't really expected to find Peck there, but she was still disappointed. The other thing she hadn't expected was the No Trespassing sign that now hung from the gate. She was sure that hadn't been there the other day. *God damn you Peck, what the hell are you up to?* As she stood at the head of the old logging road fuming, she was tempted to grab her backpack and water bottle and hike out to wherever the trail led and bring Pierce back. She only got as far as the backseat of her car before she realized that it was a terrible idea. *It's late afternoon and I have no idea where Peck dropped Pierce off. He could be anywhere. All I know is that it was on a lake. I'll wind up stuck in the woods without food or shelter when the sun goes down.*

She tried to use her phone to find a motel until she remembered there was no service. There was no way she had come all this way just to have a good cry and then drive back the same day. She was determined to stay at least one night, so she went looking for a place where her phone would work. *Thank God*, she thought when she finally got a single bar on her phone. *There's a motel in Tinkers Falls.* That would save her an hour's drive back to the Maple Inn.

When she found it and pulled in, the first thing she saw was Peck's pickup. The empty trailer he had used to haul the ATV was parked next to it. One of the wheels had been taken off to prevent anyone from stealing it. *There you are you bastard. Now I'll get some answers.*

After checking in she wanted to pound on each door until she found Peck's room and demand what was going on, but decided it might be better to just watch from her room until he showed up. Then she could decide how to approach him.

She hadn't been waiting twenty minutes when a guy came out of one of the units and got into the truck. *What the hell? That's not Peck. Who's this idiot?* As soon as he was in the truck and backing up, Katie left her room to follow him, hoping he'd lead her to Peck.

When she pulled out of the lot, she was so intent on following him that she never noticed the Bigfoot Museum right next door to the motel. The pickup only went a half mile before pulling into a family restaurant. Katie pulled in behind it and followed the guy inside. She hadn't realized how hungry she was until the smells of cooking food hit her. She took a booth where she could keep an eye on the guy and waited for a server. When she came, she was a young woman who looked to be no older than Katie was.

She placed a glass of water and a menu on the table in front of Katie. "Do you know what you want, or do you need a menu?"

"I'll look at the menu. Do you have any specials?"

"Fisherman's Platter. It's got beer-battered cod, shrimp, scallops and fries."

Katie shuddered. She didn't mind fried food, just not that much all at once. "I'll pass on that. Let me see what else is on here."

"No problem. I'll give you a couple of minutes and I'll be back."

Before she could leave, Katie nodded at the guy she had followed from the motel, "Do you know who the guy at the counter is?"

The girl gave Katie an appraising look, leaned over and whispered, "You can do better than him, honey."

"What?" Katie blushed and then replied. "Oh … no. It's just that he's driving that pickup outside and I'm looking for the owner."

The girl laughed and said, "Believe me, you can do *a lot better* than that one."

"Oh, I see you've met him."

"Yeah, he was in last night and this morning. He told me to check out his Facebook page. Apparently he's got some guy camping out in the woods on some sort of dare and he's been screwing around with him. He thinks it's funny, but it's not. Not here at least."

Katie hadn't seen Peck's post yet, but she didn't like the sound of that. "Why not here?"

"People disappear in the woods around here. Some folks say it's Bigfoot but I think that's bullshit," she answered before leaving Katie to look over the menu.

Katie watched her walk away and suddenly realized she had lost her appetite. *I have to eat though. If I don't I'll be famished tonight.* When the waitress came back, she ordered an open-faced turkey sandwich with gravy, mashed potatoes and cranberry sauce.

While she was waiting for her order, she studied the guy at the counter. He was taller than Peck, but not as tall as Pierce. He had mouse brown hair tied up in a man bun, and what he probably thought was a beard. To her it looked like a pathetic attempt to look cool. Unlike Peck, his too-pale skin was unmarked by acne. *Probably spends his time playing video games,* she thought as she watched his fingers race over his phone.

When her food came, the aroma wafting up from the plate made her stomach growl. While she ate, her thoughts bounced back and forth between Pierce, Peck and the guy who was driving Peck's pickup. Her mood cycled between worried, pissed off and confused. *I have no idea what I'm going to do, but I need to do something. I need a plan.*

Watching Peck's buddy fiddle with his phone reminded her that she hadn't been online all day. As much as she hated to, she logged on to Facebook to see what Peck had posted today.

I've been talking to the folks up here. Half of them swear Bigfoot is real and that people have disappeared in the woods where Chambers is. The other half insist it's all a load of bull to attract tourists. Chambers has a Sat-phone. Maybe I should call him and see if he's seen one yet. I don't know what to believe, but I sure wouldn't want to run into this guy in the woods. Especially if he was hungry!

The post was accompanied by another picture of the Bigfoot replica. The comments that followed ran the gamut from amused to concerned … and some were really nasty. While she was watching, another post popped up. At the same time, the guy at the counter put down his phone and laughed.

It would probably spit him out cause he'd taste like crap after a week in the woods.

That asshole just posted that, Katie thought, and stared daggers at his back.

She looked up from her phone when the waitress came with the bill. "Do you know where the Bigfoot Museum is?"

"Yeah, it's right up the road, next to the Birch Motel. You can't miss it."

"Oh, thanks. I must have driven right past it."

Bigfoot Museum. The sign wasn't huge, but it was hard to miss. She was amazed that she had driven right by it without noticing it. *I hope they're still open*, she thought as she pulled into the motel parking lot.

The door was locked when she tried to open it, but a Ring Bell for Service sign on the door looked promising so she reached out and pushed the button. When she didn't hear anything she was about to leave when a smiling woman came hustling toward her. "Hang on, I'm coming," she called, shaking a set of keys at her.

Katie waited as she unlocked the door and stepped aside. "It's ten dollars," she told her once they were both inside. From what she could see, Katie she wasn't sure it was worth ten bucks but that didn't matter. She had to see what was there, so she dug into her wallet and took out two fives.

"My name's Ms. Hickman, but you can call me Laura. If you have any questions, just ask," the woman told her.

The seven-foot Bigfoot statue dominated the room. Seeing it up close was much scarier than a picture on Peck's Facebook page. The thing dwarfed her and gave her the chills. Just the possibility of one of these being out in the woods with Pierce terrified her.

She was standing in front of it when the woman walked up behind her. "Would you like me to take a picture of you and Bigfoot?"

"No," she answered, emphatically, quickly stepping away from it to peruse the rest of the exhibits.

"Do you think it's real?" she asked as she toured the exhibits.

"Of course I do. We've had Bigfoot sightings here for hundreds of years. The Indians even had legends about him. They called him Pomoola."

"Is he … dangerous?"

"Well, that's an interesting question. Some say he is. Some say he isn't. Me, I think he's both. As long as you leave him alone, he'll leave you alone. But, if you mess with him … well, I don't think that's a good idea."

"The waitress at the diner said people disappear around here. Is that true?"

"Not for a long time. But yeah, people have disappeared around here. There were a bunch back in the thirties and one or two since then, but not in a long time."

"Then why did she say … "

"Local legend. Folks around here grow up hearing about people going missing and they get into it, ya know?"

"So if someone was camping out there it wouldn't be a problem, right!"

The woman gave her a queer look before answering. "Out where?"

"By some lake at the end of an old logging road about five miles outside of town."

"That road's blocked off. No one's supposed to use it. Why would anyone be camping out there?"

"It was a dare," Katie answered, and then told her all about it. And showed her Peck's Facebook page.

"He shouldn't be out there. Someone should tell him that."

Katie left the museum determined to do something. She had no idea what it was, so she returned to the motel where she spent a restless night filled with dreams of Pierce, Peck and Bigfoot.

Day 9 – 1

I've got to get out of here, Pierce thought when the sun finally drove away the night. His nerves were frayed from the night before. The effects of the mushroom had worn off, but he was still edgy. Something had been out in the darkness. Probably only a bear … but he still couldn't bring himself to stay where he was. He needed to be out from under the confines of the tarp and his stone enclave. Once they had offered shelter and security; now they seemed to close in on him like a trap. Even the trees overhead felt too confining. He needed to see the sun and open sky. He took his bow, arrows and knife, vowing to never go anywhere without them again. Before leaving he grabbed the camera and a fistful of jerky to assuage his hunger.

He tried to keep it together, walking at first, but soon he was running … running to get away from the terrors of the night. *The marsh. I need to get to the marsh, away from all these trees. I need sunlight and open sky!*

When he finally broke out of the trees and onto the old logging road his heart was racing and his lungs burning. He dropped the bow and arrows, bent over, placed his hands on his knees and sucked in great gulps of air.

After his heart rate had returned to normal he took one of the pieces of jerky from his pocket and ripped a chunk of it off with his teeth. *Now what? I can't just stand around here. I have to do something.* He was tempted to say, "fuck it" and start walking back to town. He turned on the camera and pointed it up the road. "This is it. I've had enough, I'm getting out of here."

He had actually taken a few steps before stopping and

chiding himself. *You were stupid. You ate a bad mushroom. You were hallucinating. Don't do it again and you'll be alright. Now pull yourself together and get on with it.*

"Sorry, I've changed my mind. I can still do this. I've got the bow and arrows so I might as well try to find something to eat. Some fresh meat would be welcome," he told the camera. *And, even if I don't find anything, it's something to do.*

"So, let's see what's on the other side of the marsh. I've got to be careful not to step into the water. The last time I did that I sank up to my knees in mud. You saw what happened, I was covered in leeches and it smelled terrible. I don't want to do that again."

When he reached the far side of the marsh he found exactly what he had thought he might, woods that were no different than the ones he had just left. "Surprise, more woods, but since I'm here I might as well do some exploring," he said, and made his way along the shore of the lake.

He had been walking for an hour when he came across the remains of a whitetail deer. "What the hell happed here?" he asked as he panned the camera at it. The animal had been savaged and the area surrounding it looked as if a battle had been fought there.

Pierce felt his gorge rise when he got closer to the corpse. The head had been crushed and the brain was missing. A blood-stained rock lay a few feet away. The skin was ripped open in several places and chunks of meet had been torn, or bitten, from the underlying flesh.

"What kind of animal could have done this? Not a bear. A bear couldn't crack the skull open with a rock." Then he remembered the signs for the Bigfoot Museum. *No way,* he thought, but his skin still crawled at the possibility. The thing he had seen in the night couldn't have been real. It was a product of fear and the mushrooms. It had to be.

Then he realized the woods had gone silent. Not a bird sang, not a squirrel or chipmunk scurried through the fallen leaves on the forest floor. Before he had come to live out here he never would have noticed the unnatural stillness. Now it struck him like a blow and the hair stood up on his arms and the back of his neck. Any thought of going on evaporated. All he wanted to do was get back to the familiar confines of his camp. Irrational as it might be, he felt safe there. Before heading back, though, he strung his bow and nocked an arrow. It might not be much of a deterrent, but it was all he had.

"I'm getting away from here," he said before turning the camera off.

When he reached the marsh he felt even more vulnerable than he had in the woods. The weed and cattail choked water on his left felt like a confining barrier he could hardly see through. As he picked his away along its edge he had to continuously glance down to check his footing. During those few seconds he was sure something was going to pounce upon him. He finally placed the arrow back in its mount so he had a free hand for his hunting knife.

By time he reached the old logging road his nerves were frayed. *The hell with the challenge, I'm going to make the call and tell Peck to come and get me. Staying out here just isn't worth it.*

Peck woke with the sun. He was really looking forward to this day. Last night Chambers had seen him in the Bigfoot costume. Today would be more of the same. But first, breakfast, the thought made all the sweeter by knowing it was something Chambers wasn't going to have. This morning it was bacon and eggs, baked beans, brown bread and coffee. He was just sitting down to eat when some movement in the woods caught his eye. He stopped with the fork halfway to his mouth.

He sat like that, frozen in place, watching for something, any movement. It didn't come. Not until he took his first sip of coffee. Then there was a hint of motion. It was as if something in the background shifted.

What the hell is out there? A bear? No, I don't think it's a bear. Bears are black. I don't see any black out there. Maybe it's nothing, just the wind.

Peck finished eating, but he couldn't shake the feeling that something was watching him. *Damn, Chambers is the one who's supposed to be getting spooked, not me. I've got to quit this shit and get on to taking care of him.*

As soon as he was done eating, Peck grabbed the Bigfoot suit, climbed onto the ATV and headed toward Chambers. Once he was gone, the thing that had been watching him came out of hiding.

The old road was starting to show the effects of Peck's travels. Wheel tracks and beaten down grass and weeds made it evident the trail had seen a lot of recent use. *It's a good thing Chambers can't see this. He'd know someone is out here with him.*

Once Peck arrived at his normal parking spot he changed out of his clothes and into the Bigfoot costume. Within minutes he was sweating like a pig. There was no help for that, not if he wanted to be sure Chambers didn't see him carrying the thing under his arm. He couldn't even take the head off. He had only gone half a mile and sweat was trickling into his eyes. And there was no way to wipe it away without removing the headpiece. *Maybe this isn't such a great idea. I should go back and wait until later in the day when it's not so hot to do this.*

He started to turn around, but then chided himself for being a pussy. *Just do it. You have a plan, so stick to it.* He did, however, take the headpiece off. He'd put it back on when he got closer.

The headpiece went on as soon as he saw the marsh at the end of the road. He'd seen Chambers there several times. He squatted low to stay off the horizon until he was sure Chambers wasn't in the area. Then he cautiously made his way down the road toward the point where he would veer off it toward the prick's camp site.

Walking on the road had been fairly easy, but it took all his concentration once he was off it and into the woods. Roots threatened to trip him and his costume continuously caught on branches and bushes. At the first sight of Chambers' camp, he hunkered down and looked for his adversary. After twenty minutes, when nothing moved in the camp, he decided it was safe to get closer.

Time to mess with your head, Adventure Boy. Let's see how you like this.

It took less than twenty minutes for Peck to destroy Chambers' camp. He tore down the tarp, scattered his belongings and ripped his sleeping bag apart. The last thing he did before heading back toward his own camp was smash the Sat-phone. *Screw him, if he wants out, he's going to have to walk back to the main road.*

Day 9 – 2

Pierce stopped before stepping onto the old logging road. *I'm going to be totally exposed once I step out of these trees, so I'd better see what's out there before I do.* At first he was sure the road was empty, but then he saw it, a large, hairy figure walking upright. It was only there for a minute or two and then disappeared over the horizon. *Holy crap, it's real.*

As soon as it was gone, he hurried across the road and into the trees. He had to get back to his camp and the Sat-phone. He wanted out of here now!

Pierce broke through the trees and stopped short when he got the first glimpse of his camp. *What? What the hell happened?* The state it was in staggered him. His heart started racing and he was on the verge of panic. The violence of the slaughtered deer, the ruin of his camp, the thing on the road; he needed to get out before it was too late.

"Oh, no," he cried when he saw the open lid of the box containing the cameras and Sat-phone. All hope of help from the outside lay scattered about him in pieces. The cameras were untouched, but that didn't help him. It was the phone he needed. Overwhelmed, he sank to his knees and stared hopelessly at the ruins of what he had hoped would be his salvation.

Pierce didn't know how long he sat staring out at the woods, but when he finally got to his feet, his mind was made up … he was going to walk out. And he was going to start now. He hadn't gone ten yards when he stopped and turned back. *Don't be stupid. Take the axe and the rest of the jerky. You might need those.*

"First the deer and now this," Pierce said as he panned the

camera across his ruined campsite. "I can't stay here any longer. I don't know who's doing this, but it's getting worse. I'm out of here. A silly bet isn't worth getting killed by some psycho."

This time when he left the camp he was as well-armed as he could be. He was carrying the bow in one hand and the axe in the other. A camera was strapped to his chest. He wasn't sure how much good the bow or the axe would do him, but they were better than nothing. They had to be … didn't they? He wanted to run, but fought the urge. That was all he needed to do, run blindly into the thing he was trying to escape. Instead, he crept through the woods, jumping at every sound and movement, no matter how benign he knew them to be.

He flinched and dropped to the ground when a blue jay's raucous call sounded from above. The damn things were the wood's warning system, crying out at intruders. "Go away," he hissed, but the bird didn't listen. Instead, it sat in the branches above him and announced his presence to any creature within the range of its voice. To make things worse, it was joined by two of its brethren who also took up the call. Since they seemed determined to stay and make a racket above him, Pierce gave up and started walking. To his chagrin, the jays followed along, continuing their raucous calls. They didn't leave him until he broke out of the trees at the old logging road.

The fear that had gripped him faded under the cloudless expanse of the open sky. The axe that he had been carrying since he left camp felt heavier than it should and his hand cramped from gripping it. He couldn't imagine carrying it all the way back to the parking area where Peck had dropped him. Reluctantly, he dropped it in the center of the road and walked away from it. All he had to protect himself now was the bow, the hunting knife and his wits. He hoped they would be enough.

He had only gone a half mile when he saw the creature coming toward him down the road.

Peck was still laughing to himself when he rounded the bend where the ATV was parked. *I wish I could see Chambers' face when he finds what I did. That should send him packing.* The laughter stuck in his throat when he realized the ATV was gone. "Shit," he swore and ran toward the spot where he had left it. Then he saw it, and his heart sank. Someone had pushed it off the road and into a deep ditch.

It had to be Chambers, that asshole. Who else is out here? He must have seen me and found it.

When he reached the ATV he realized that Chambers had done more than just push it into the ditch. It was upside down, the seats were torn out of it and all the wires from the engine were missing. There was no way he was ever going to get it out of the ditch and drive it in that condition. To make matters worse, if they could be worse, he could just see one leg of his pants sticking out from beneath the frame. He tried to pull them out, but they wouldn't budge. His shirt was nowhere to be found. Unless he wanted to strip down to his underwear and feed the horseflies and mosquitoes he was stuck in the Bigfoot suit.

Screw that, I'll change when I get back to camp. I don't need this, though, he thought and dropped the costume's head on the road.

The walk back took longer walking than it had riding. By the time he got there he was hot, sweaty and tired. *I need a beer,* he thought as he turned off the main logging road onto the side trail that led to his camp. All hopes of a cold one died when he discovered the wreckage that had been his camp. Huge holes had been torn in the tent, equipment was strewn everywhere. The cooler was torn open and empty, all the food and beer gone. *Chambers. That asshole! He wasn't supposed to go this far from the lake.*

Things were worse inside the tent. Both cots were in pieces and the sleeping bags shredded. Even the floor had huge tears in it. There was nothing here he could save.

Then he realized what was missing. *Shit, where the hell are my clothes?*

It didn't take long to find them, but now they were nothing more than rags. They had been ripped and torn past any hope of being worn.

"Fuck," he swore. The only thing he had left was the costume and the underwear he was wearing.

When he finally got done cursing at Chambers, he realized what a bind he was in. He was miles from the end of the logging road, which was miles from town. He had no food or water, and he was stuck in a Bigfoot costume. Even Chambers was better off than he was. He at least had clothes, water, fire and food.

Well, I'd better start walking, he finally admitted. *The longer I wait the longer it's going to take me.*

When he reached the logging road, he stood for a minute looking back toward Chambers' camp. He'd love to have it out with the asshole, but physically he was no match for the prick.

"Fuck you, Chambers. I'll be back." He had a long walk ahead of him, so he turned left toward town. *There's no way I'm staying out here after today. Chambers is on his own. That asshole can rot out here for all I care.*

Peck felt the presence before he saw it. The hairs on his neck stood out and his skin felt like it was covered with crawling insects. Some primal instinct told him to stop where he was, or better yet, turn and run.

"Stop it. There's nothing to be afraid of," he said out loud just to break the unnatural silence. He hadn't gone ten yards when a thing straight out of a bad acid trip stepped out of the woods and onto the road in front of him. He froze in place. *What the hell is that?* He knew instinctively it was not a man in a costume. This was the real thing … a Bigfoot.

If the one in the museum was scary, this one was terrifying. It was taller and more massive. It was at least eight feet tall and covered in coarse red fur. Its chest was wide and deep, its arms impossibly long, with hands the size of dinner plates. One of them could easily fit around his skull like his hand could grip a grapefruit.

They stood there on the road, neither one moving. Peck wanted to run, but he was frozen in place until the creature snarled and took a step toward him. When it threw back its head and roared, he saw long, yellowed canines that could rip an animal apart. Peck's bladder let go and a warm stream of urine ran down his leg and soaked into the costume that was already damp from sweat. Then the creature pointed back down the road toward the marsh. That was all it took to release Peck from his paralysis. He turned and fled back in the direction he had been coming from.

Peck ran in a blind panic until the pain in his side forced him to stop. As he stood bent over sucking wind, he risked a glance behind him. The monster was still there, twenty yards away, watching him. It wasn't even breathing hard. Running had gained him nothing.

It stood motionless until Peck managed to straighten up. Then it growled, showing him those awful teeth, and took a menacing step toward him. When Peck failed to move it roared and rushed three enormous steps closer. Despite the pain in his side, Peck managed to shuffle away from it, moving further down the old logging road toward the marsh where he had abandoned Chambers that first day. Every time he dared a backward glance, the creature was there, trailing behind him.

When Peck walked, it walked. When he stopped, it stopped. *It's herding me*, he realized once his panic dropped to a level where he could think. *But where does it want me to go?*

When they passed the ATV, the creature grunted and bent down to retrieve the head Peck had discarded. It held it out for Peck to see, then roared, ripped it in half and threw the pieces into the ditch. Then it pointed toward the lake. It was a frightening sign that the creature was intelligent and that it wanted him to keep moving.

Peck considered jumping off the old road and running but knew he could never outrun the monster in the woods. The only option he had was to keep on walking. He hadn't gone much further when he saw Chambers. He had never thought he'd be glad to see that guy. Chambers was carrying a bow and it was strung and ready to go. Peck was about to run to him when he remembered he was wearing the Bigfoot costume. *Shit, he'll shoot me sure as hell if I just start running toward him.* Instead, he waved his arms and yelled.

"Chambers, don't shoot! It's me, Peck!"

He saw the shock on Chambers' face when he looked past him and saw the monster following him down the road.

"Chambers, don't shoot! It's me, Peck!" he yelled again, and then started running.

"Shoot it. Kill it!" he demanded when Chambers just stood there staring at the thing. Instead of shooting the creature, the idiot lowered the bow and turned on him, demanding to know what the hell was going on and why he was in the costume.

Katie rolled over in bed and glanced at the clock on the bedside table. *It's nine o'clock. I didn't mean to sleep so late. I've got to get moving.*

She hopped out of bed and went directly to the room's window to check the parking lot. She breathed a sigh of relief when she saw Peck's pickup in the same place it had been last night.

If I hurry I probably have time for a shower. I should have taken one before I went to bed, but I didn't think of it.

Twenty minutes later she was showered and dressed, but her hair was still wet. Before drying it she peeked out the window. The pickup was gone.

"Damn, damn, damn," she swore as she grabbed her keys and rushed out the door. "I've got to find him. Maybe he's at the diner."

To her relief, the pickup was parked outside the diner when she got there. She took the spot next to it and went inside to see if she could find out anything about what Peck was up to.

When she walked in, Stanley was seated alone in a booth. *Here goes nothing*, she thought and slid onto the seat across from him. Stanley almost choked on his coffee and then fought to recover his composure. "Uh, can I help you?"

"Maybe. Is that your pickup outside?"

Stanley looked outside and then back at her. "Yeah, why?"

"Because it looks like a friend of mine's, Michael Peck. You know him?"

"You know Mike?"

"Yeah. That is his truck, isn't it?"

Stanley's eyes grew suspicious. "How did you know we were up here? Mike didn't say anything about a girl." Then he caught on. "Hey you're Chambers' girlfriend. What are you doing up here?"

"No, what are *you* doing up here and where's Peck? You guys are messing with Pierce, aren't you?"

Stanley got quiet and didn't answer.

"Fine," Katie said and used her cell phone to snap his picture.

"What was that for," Stanley demanded

"Peck's Facebook page. I've got pictures of you and the truck outside the motel. I'm sure all his followers would love to know that he's rigging the game."

"You can't do that."

"Sure I can ... unless you tell me exactly what Peck is up to." She intended to post it anyway, but he didn't have to know that.

Stanley squirmed in his seat before answering. Then he seemed to become sure of himself. "We're not messing with him, we're staying close so we can be there if he calls on the Sat-phone."

"Really?" She doubted it, but it could be the truth. "So where, exactly, is Peck?"

Stanley looked like he didn't want to answer, but Katie pushed him. "Where is he?"

"We have a camp about two miles from his. Mike checks on him every day to make sure he's doing okay."

Katie wasn't sure if she believed him. Not after meeting Peck and reading his posts. He hated Pierce.

"I want to see this camp for myself."

"Sorry. You can't. It's too far to walk and Mike's got the ATV. He'll be back in two days. You can talk to him then if you want to stick around."

"Fine. I will," Katie agreed, but she wasn't happy about it. In the meantime she was going to keep an eye on this asshole.

She was just about to leave the booth when the waitress appeared. "Can I get you something? Coffee?"

"Coffee and a menu," Katie answered and then moved to another booth, one where she could keep an eye on Stanley. She needn't have bothered because he left without finishing his breakfast. He just dropped some cash on the table and split.

Lying bastard, Katie thought as she watched through the

window as he got into the pickup and drove away. *After break-fast I'm going out there and see for myself.*

The No Trespassing sign on the gate pissed her off all over again when she saw it. *Pierce never would have gone out there if he had seen that sign. That's why Peck took it down. He put it back up so no one else would go out there.*

Standing at the gate, Katie realized just how powerless she was. She had no idea where Peck had dropped Pierce off or where his campsite was. Even if she started walking now, she might never find him. *I wish I would have asked him for the sat-phone number. I could have called and told him Peck's out there. I have to wait. But I'll be here when he gets back. That's for sure.*

Day 9 – 3

Pierce didn't think … he just reacted. He had an arrow nocked and was starting to pull it back when he realized the creature running toward him was waving its arm and calling his name.

"Chambers, don't shoot! It's me, Peck!"

It took Pierce a minute to realize what was happening. He already had the arrow drawn and was ready to release it when he recognized Peck. Anger exploded in his head. *Son of a bitch, that asshole! He's been fucking with me. I ought to shoot his ass.* Then he saw the creature that was following in Peck's wake. This one was huge, and it made Peck's costume look like exactly what it was, a cheap imitation. A spike of fear shot through him. Could this one be real?

Pierce held the arrow at full draw but didn't release it. If he did he might actually hit Peck. And, he couldn't be sure the thing following him wasn't just another asshole in a better costume.

Peck was shaking when he stumbled to Pierce's feet. "Shoot it! Kill it!"

Pierce eyed the creature. It had stopped about forty yards from where they were and was staring at them across the distance. Pierce lowered the bow and un-nocked the arrow. The creature was too far away for a shot. It must have known it, because it just stood there and stared at them. Instead, he reached down and grabbed Peck by the collar of the costume and dragged him to his feet.

"What the hell's going on Peck? What are you doing in that costume and who, or what, is that thing on the road?"

Peck didn't answer. He just stared back up the road shaking, his eyes wide with fear. He didn't calm down until the creature turned and walked back the way they had come. When it was gone, he turned to Pierce and started babbling. Everything came out in a rush. "It tore my camp apart. It destroyed my ATV and herded me here. I don't know what it wants."

"What the hell are you doing out here in the first place?"

Peck was at a loss for an answer until Pierce let him go by shoving him backward. "I was here for you," he said when he landed on his ass. "If anything happened I needed to be close enough to evacuate you if I needed to."

"Right. And that's why you smashed the sat-phone? That's bullshit and we both know it. Well, fuck you Peck. I'm leaving. The bet's off." Pierce stepped around Peck and started walking up the road toward civilization.

"Wait, what about me? Don't leave me here!" Peck called to his back.

"I don't really care. Do whatever you want."

Peck quickly scrambled to his feet. "Then I'm coming with you."

"Fine … keep up if you can and don't get in the way. I'm not waiting for you."

Peck tried to keep up, but Chambers' longer legs and the awkwardness of the costume combined to slow the smaller man down. Pierce was soon ten yards in front of him and getting further away by the minute. Then he abruptly stopped in his tracks. The creature had come back and was standing in the road ahead of them. It was far enough away not to be a danger. He didn't even bother nocking an arrow, but he had no doubt it could close the distance between them in an instant.

When Pierce took a step toward the creature it roared at him and pointed back the way he had come, making it obvious it wanted them to turn around and go back. Pierce wasn't happy about it, but he did it. As soon as he did an about-face, the creature stepped off the road and back into the woods.

"Where are you going?" Peck demanded when Pierce turned back and walked past him.

"Back to my camp, or what's left of it, thanks to you."

"I'm coming with you. I'm not staying out here alone."

Pierce thought about telling him to fuck off, that he was on his own, but couldn't bring himself to do it. The guy was an asshole, but he couldn't abandon him to face the creature alone.

"Fine, keep up if you can. If not, I'm sure you know how to find it. And pick up the axe I dropped on the way. We'll need it."

When he got back to the camp Pierce looked at the wreckage and took a seat on the log he used as a chair. Peck arrived ten minutes later carrying the axe. "You did this, so I suggest you get to work putting things back in order."

"What are you going to do?" Peck demanded.

Pierce held the bow in front of Peck's face. "I'm going to stand guard."

Pierce watched as Peck gathered the equipment and wood he had scattered about the camp. He jumped at every sound from the surrounding woods. "You'd better get the tarp back up because that's where you're sleeping tonight," he said when Peck looked like he was going to take a break.

"Why can't I sleep up there with you?"

"You're kidding, right? It's a small space and I'm not about to share it. If you want to be dry if it rains, you'd better get to it."

Peck struggled, but managed to get the tarp back up in some semblance of its former shape. When he was done, Pierce directed him to gather firewood and kindling for a fire. Once he did that, Pierce used the ferro rod to start a fire.

Pierce stared at Peck across the fire, getting more pissed with every minute. "Tell me about your plan Peck. Who's in on it with you?"

"No one," Peck lied.

"Bullshit. You wouldn't do this all by yourself. So who's helping you?"

"Stanley," Peck finally answered. "I stay for three days and he comes out for one."

"Was that him in the other costume?"

"What? No. Derick's not due back for two days. That thing was real. It trashed my camp and my ATV. Then it forced me to come here."

"What did you do?"

"Nothing. It just tore everything up and then it wouldn't let me leave. I don't know why."

"You call sneaking over here in the night, making animal noises from up there, kicking stuff down on my camp and wearing a Bigfoot costume to spook me, *nothing*? I know it had to be you."

"That was all harmless," Peck said, trying to defend himself, and confirming Pierce's suspicions.

"And then you tried to leave. What were you going to do, just abandon me here to deal with that thing on my own?"

"I was going to get help," Peck replied, but Pierce knew he was lying. He'd have been long gone if he could have.

"I'm tempted to throw you out of here … but I'm not going to. The two of us …." Then he stopped and cocked his head. "Quiet, listen," he told Peck.

They both stood, listening until Peck said, "What? I don't hear anything."

"Exactly. It's too quiet. No crows or blue jays squawking in the trees, no squirrels or chipmunks skittering through the leaves, nothing. That thing is out there. It's watching us."

Peck seemed to shrink into himself as he peered into the trees. "What are we going to do?"

Pierce shrugged. "Nothing. What can we do?"

Peck started to say something, and then stopped. Pierce was right. There wasn't anything they could do. They were trapped here.

As the sun set and the woods darkened, Peck peered into the shadows and wished he had the night-vision glasses he had used every other time he had come here in the dark. He almost jumped out of his skin when a ghostly cry came from the lake.

"Relax, Peck, it's only a loon," Chambers said from his place under the rock shelf.

Peck wasn't sure, but he thought he heard amusement in

his voice. The prick was laughing at him. "You think this is funny, Chambers?" he demanded.

"This? No. You? Yes. Payback is a bitch. It's ironic, don't you think? You wanted to scare me into quitting and now you're stuck out here with me."

He didn't think it was funny. No, not at all. "Yeah, well what are we going to do tonight?" he demanded.

"What do you think we're going to do? We're going to stay here near the fire and try to get some sleep. Tomorrow we can try to make our way back to town."

"What about something to eat? Have you got anything?" he asked, hoping Chambers would have something. He was starving.

"Look around, Peck. Do you see anything?"

He didn't, but he didn't trust Chambers either. "There must be something. What have you been eating? What about the rice and jerky you brought with you?"

"I find my food every day, just like the contestants on the show. If you want to eat, you can do the same thing. But, if you're really hungry, you can have some rice. All you have to do is walk down to the lake and get some water so we can cook it."

"Are you crazy? I'm not going out there in the dark. Why didn't you say something before? We could have gotten it then."

"I was thinking about other things then. Like what you did to my camp. As far as I'm concerned you can starve out here."

"Wait, we're in this together now. We have to help each other."

"We're not in it together Peck. We're here together, but we're not a team. You're going to have to fend for yourself."

"Look, Chambers, I'm sorry. It was a shitty thing to do. But this is different. We could die out here if we don't work together."

When Chambers didn't answer he wondered if he really had gone too far. *Is he really willing to abandon me out here if he gets the chance?*

"Fine," Chambers finally answered. "But when we get back you're going on Facebook and Twitter to tell everyone exactly what you did out here."

"Okay," Peck agreed. Hell, he'd agree to anything right now.

That didn't mean he had to actually do it once they got back.

"As a matter of fact, I think it's confession time. They say it's good for the soul." Chambers told him.

"What do you mean, confession time?"

Chambers held up the camera and started filming. "Hey, everybody. Look who I met out here … my good friend Mike Peck. Mike, why don't you tell everyone exactly what you've been doing out here?

"Well?" Chambers said when he didn't answer.

"I'm not going to do that."

"Fine, then leave."

That asshole, he knows I can't leave.

"What do you want me to say?" he finally asked.

"Tell them what you've been up to out here."

You prick. I'll get you for this, he thought before he started talking. "I've been out here screwing around with Chambers. I came over in the night and made a bunch of animal noises on the ridge above his camp to try and scare him."

"That's a start. Now tell them what you did to my camp."

"I came over here today and messed it up."

"Now tell them why you're wearing that costume and what happened next. I'm interested in this part myself."

Peck glared at Chambers before answering. If looks could indeed kill, the prick would have a massive heart attack on the spot. "I got this costume to scare Chambers into quitting. I came here today but he was gone, so I messed up his camp. On my way back to my camp I found my ATV upside down in a ditch. All the wires had been torn out. When I walked back to my campsite, it had been torn apart too. When I tried to leave, a real Bigfoot wouldn't let me. It drove me here."

"That sounds like a load of crap, doesn't it?" Chambers commented. "But I saw it too. So now, here we are, stuck out in these woods with a thing I never really believed existed. And it's all this asshole's fault. I just wish I had had the sense to get it on tape. If I don't, no one will ever believe this."

"My fault? How is this my fault? If you hadn't bragged about how you could so do this we wouldn't be out here."

"Right, but if you hadn't been so intent on fucking with me

you wouldn't be here, would you? You have nobody to blame for this but yourself."

He wasn't about to admit Chambers was right, so Peck didn't respond. Then he remembered that Chambers had also brought beef jerky in his emergency rations.

"What about that beef jerky you brought? Do you have any of that left?"

"Yeah, but I'm saving that. Going hungry for one night's not going to kill you. I know. I go to sleep hungry every night."

Screw him. He goes to bed hungry every night. He must think that makes him some kind of hero. He's probably going to sit up there and eat jerky where I can't see him.

They sat in silence as the night wore on. He was startled when Chambers announced he was going to sleep.

"Give me the bow and arrows in case that thing attacks," Peck said.

"I don't think so. I don't trust you enough for that. Keep the fire going and call me if anything happens. Oh, and I'll take the axe, too. I'll feel safer if it's up there with me," Chambers told him.

Peck dared not fall asleep. He couldn't even if he wanted to. That thing was out there. If he let the fire go out who knew what it would do. As the night wore on, and he heard Chambers' even breathing as he slept, his hatred for him grew. *Asshole. He's got all the weapons and he's tucked up under that rock like some king in his castle while I'm stuck out here in the open. If we get out of here I'm really going to fuck him.*

DAY 10

Peck's pickup wasn't in the parking lot when Katie peeked out through the curtain of her room. It wasn't at the diner either when she stopped in for breakfast.

"Has that guy I was talking to yesterday been in yet this morning?" she asked the waitress when she came for her order.

"Nope, haven't seen him since yesterday. I think you spooked him."

So where is he? Did he take off to join Peck out in the woods? I'd better get out there to find out.

"Can I get an egg and cheese sandwich on a hard roll and a large black coffee to go?" she asked the waitress.

"Sure. I'll put that right in for you. Is that all you want?"

"For now, yes, but I'll probably be back later."

When the sandwich and coffee came, Katie took the bag to her car and headed out to the head of the old logging trail. She had no idea what she was going to do when she got there. That would depend on whether the pickup was there or not.

Damn, he's not here. The spot was as deserted now as it had been the day before. The bright yellow No Trespassing sign with its bold black letters was still there and it pissed her off all over again. *What had Peck been thinking when he sent Pierce off to survive on his own in an area that was clearly off limits? There had to be a reason it was posted. Had Peck even looked into why, or did he just not care?*

Katie sat in the car for over two hours. During that entire time not one car passed by. She was about to get out to pee in the woods when she saw a pickup kicking up a rooster tail of dust approaching in her rearview mirror. She thought it might be Peck's until she noticed it was the wrong color. It slowed as it came along side and she saw two rough-looking locals peering out the window at her. One of them winked and the other laughed. That was all it took to convince her she really didn't want to sit there any longer.

"Well, you're back. That's a surprise," Laura Hickman said when Katie came through the door of the Bigfoot Museum.

"Can we talk?" Katie asked.

"Of course. What would you like to talk about?"

"Bigfoot. All kidding aside, do you think it's real?"

"Why are you asking?"

"I'm worried about my boyfriend. He's somewhere out there and he thinks he's alone, but he's not. There's another guy out there messing with him. If those things are real, he could be in real trouble."

The woman thought for a moment before answering. "I tell the tourists they're real, but of course they're not."

"So all this is what, a scam?"

"No dear, it's just a bit of fun we have with the flatlanders."

"So where did all the pictures and the newspaper articles come from?"

Laura didn't answer right away. When she did, Katie thought she sounded a bit evasive. "Some folks say they've actually seen one. But they just do it to get attention. The pictures? Just men in costumes."

"Why on earth would they do that?"

"Because there's not much else to do around here. They get bored, get to drinking and out come the Bigfoot costumes."

"If I wanted to go out there to get my friend, how would I do it?"

"You'd need an ATV, and you shouldn't go alone. Is there anyone you could go with?"

Katie thought of Peck and his friend, but she wasn't about to go into the woods with either of them. "No. Do you know anyone who might go with me?"

"Jeff Gibbs might do it if I ask."

"Would you, please?"

"Of course. Give me your number and I'll call and let you know if he's available."

Laura Hickman locked the door made the call as soon as the Katie left. Gibbs didn't answer, so she left a message.

Peck's pickup was still missing when she got back to the motel. With nothing else to do, she drove back to the head of the old logging road. The gate with its No Trespassing sign was still in place. Like the last time she had been there, the site was deserted. The road and the woods beyond seemed to mock her.

Pierce was lying on the remains of his sleeping bag, just past sunrise, watching Peck, who appeared to be sleeping next to the fire. *What a prick. He arranges this whole thing just so he can try and scare me into tapping out. I should just grab my stuff and leave him here.*

He was ready to do just that when he was startled by something sailing out of the sky. It landed two feet from where Peck lay sprawled on the ground. If it had been any closer, it would have struck the tarp that Peck had managed to set back up. It only took Pierce a minute to realize what it was, the body of a small deer. Its head had been crushed just like the one he had found the day before. Peck woke with a start and started screaming as soon as he saw the carcass. A guttural growl from the ledge above them shocked him into silence.

Pierce grabbed his bow and strung an arrow, but he was damned if he was going to step out from below his rock shelter. It only took a minute for Peck to scramble from his place under the tarp and into the protection provided by the overhang.

"What are you going to do?" he demanded once he was huddled next to Pierce.

"What do you mean what am I going to do? What are you going to do? You're the reason we're out here."

"I'm not ..."

"Bullshit. You'd better start coming up with some ideas or I'm going to feed you to that thing and take my chances on my own."

Peck shook his head and Pierce thought he was going to

start crying any minute. "Chambers, I'm sorry. I was wrong. We need to work together here," he practically begged.

Pathetic little wimp. He's going to be more of a hazard than a help, but I can't just leave him here. "Fine, but you do what I tell you, no arguments. Cross me once and you're on your own. Got it?"

"Got it," Peck agreed.

Right, until you get a chance to screw me that is.

They waited, listening for any movement from above. Finally, when the tension became too much, Pierce started to crawl out from beneath the overhang.

Peck grabbed his arm to stop him. "Where are you going?" he demanded

"We can't stay here all day. I'm going to see if it's still out there."

Once he was clear of the overhang, Pierce scanned the area above them. It was empty. "You can come out. It's gone," he told Peck.

"Are you sure?"

"No, but I don't see it. So get out here."

Peck didn't look happy about leaving the shelter of the overhang but he did it.

"Check out that deer. See how old it is and what condition it's in." Pierce told him as he continued to scan the woods for the creature.

"Why?" Peck asked.

"Just do it," Pierce told him. He thought he knew what Peck was going to find but he didn't want to say anything just yet.

Peck approached the deer like it was going to jump up and attack him. When he finally reached it, and nothing happened, he called back to Pierce, "Its head is bashed in but that's all."

"Turn it over," Pierce called back, keeping his eyes on the woods.

He heard Peck grunt and a minute later he got the answer he'd been expecting. "Nothing, but it's still warm."

"Right, I thought so," Pierce answered and turned to face him.

"What do you mean you thought so? What the hell is going on?"

"The creature is feeding us. It herded us back here and now it wants us to stay. I have no idea why, and I don't want to find out, but for right now I'm going to do what it wants. I'm going to eat some of that deer."

Peck stepped away from the animal with a look of horror on his face and Pierce couldn't help laughing.

"You think this is funny?" he demanded, staring daggers at Pierce.

"Not this. You and that costume. You look ridiculous."

Peck glowered at him. "It's the only thing I have to wear unless you have something I can use."

"You can have my extra pair of pants and a shirt. They'll be too big for you, but it will have to do. Before you do though, you need to get us some meat off that deer."

"What, why me?"

"Because you said you were a hunter, so you must know how to get the meat off a deer. We don't need the whole thing, just enough for a few meals. While you're doing that, I'll start a fire."

"How am I supposed to do that? I don't have a knife."

"Use this one," Pierce told him and handed him the hunting knife, handle first.

Peck took it and started on the deer. He skinned a haunch and cut a large hunk of meat from it. "How's this?" he asked, holding it out for Pierce to see.

Pierce looked at it and frowned. "It's a bit thick, don't you think? How about cutting it into two thinner pieces, say an inch thick? It'll cook a lot easier like that."

"Sure," Peck answered sullenly as he started to slice the hunk of venison into two steaks. By the time he was done, Pierce had a fire going.

"Give me the knife and I'll cut some sticks for a spit. We're going to have to cook those over the flames. I don't have a frying pan."

"I'll do it," Peck volunteered, and Pierce could tell he didn't want to give up the knife.

"Wait. It might be easier if you used the axe. Just don't cut yourself with the damn thing."

Peck took the axe, but didn't go far to find the two Y-shaped branches and a straight stick they needed to suspend the meat over the flames.

Pierce sat on the log he used for a chair watching the venison turn from blood-red to brown as it cooked over the fire. Peck was sitting on the ground. Smoke rose up from the fire along with the smell of cooking meat. Pierce found that the events of the night and the previous day hadn't dampened his appetite. If anything, they had sharpened it. His stomach was growling in anticipation.

"Have you ever had venison before?" Pierce asked while they waited for the meat to cook.

"Of course. Haven't you?" Peck answered.

"No, I never ate anything wild before this trip."

Peck started to laugh but then stopped abruptly. "You're kidding, right? I thought you were Survivor Man and all that shit."

"Nah, I just loved the idea of it. I mean, I knew I could do it, or at least I thought I could, but I never really spent any time alone living off the land before. How about you?"

"I've hunted since I was a kid so I've had venison, squirrel, rabbit and duck. It's all okay, but I'll take a good beef steak any day. Right now, though, I don't care ... venison will do just fine."

When the meat looked done, Pierce took it off the fire and waited for it to cool before sliding one of the chunks off the stick and handing it to Peck. He kept the stick with the second piece of meat for himself. He took a bite. It was a little tough and "gamey" but it was delicious.

"Any idea how long we're going to be able to eat this? Do you think it'll still be good tomorrow?" Pierce asked Peck.

"What do you mean tomorrow? We've got to get out of here."

"We can try, but I don't think we can. That thing wants us here for some reason."

"You have the bow. You can kill it."

"Are you crazy? It's only a 60 pound pull. I don't know if it could kill that thing. And, I only have three hunting arrows. The other three are target arrows. If I shoot at it and either miss it, or worse, hit it and not kill it, who knows what it will do.

Right now we appear to be safe. I'll shoot it if I have to, but I'm not going looking for trouble."

"That's ridiculous. We need to get out of here. If you're not willing to kill that thing I will. Give me the bow and I'll do it."

Pierce's first reaction was to tell him "hell no" but then changed his mind. "Fine, take it and go. But, if you do leave, don't come back. If you fuck it up I don't want it coming back on me."

Peck took the bow and arrows and started to leave. "You coming?" he asked

"Nope. I'm staying right here."

"What?"

"I said I'm staying right here."

"Without the bow and arrows?"

"Yep. I'll have the axe and knife. They may not be much, but they're better than nothing. If you manage to kill it, I'll be able to walk out. If you don't, and it kills you, maybe it will leave me alone. Either way, I like my chances better that way."

Peck frowned at him, looked at the bow and arrows, and then turned back. "I'm not going to be your fool. I'll wait and see what happens."

"Suit yourself," Pierce told him. "But if you stay, you're going to have to pull your weight around here."

"That thing should be field-dressed. In this weather this meat's going to spoil pretty quickly. I give it ten, maybe twelve hours at the most."

"Then maybe we should try smoking some of it," Pierce suggested. "Have you ever done that?"

"Nope, and we don't have a smoker, so I don't know how we'd be able to do it."

"Me either," Pierce agreed. "I saw it done on one of the shows. They cut the meat in thin strips and hung it over the fire and used wet wood to make the smoke. I just don't think I'd trust myself to do it right, so we should eat what we can today."

"Well, we can cook some anyway and at least try to smoke some," Peck suggested.

"Fine. You cut the meat and we'll give it a try."

Peck cut several long strips from the deer's hind leg. When he was done, Pierce hung them over the fire and threw old leaves and moss on the flames. Acrid-smelling smoke filled the air and engulfed the meat.

"I've never smoked anything before, any idea how long we have to keep this up?" Peck asked just before a slight gust of wind blew the smoke directly in his face. Pierce had to stifle a laugh when he backed away coughing and waving his arms in front of his face.

They smoked the meat for several hours, watching it shrivel and turn from red to brown. "Try a piece and see what you think," Pierce suggested.

"Why me?" Peck demanded.

"Oh, fine, I'll try it. I'm not trying to kill you Peck. I was just offering you the first piece."

Pierce lifted a strip off the stick they had hung it over, waited for it to cool, and then took a bite. It was well done, brown all the way through. "It's tough, but I can taste the smoke. Let's hope it's okay."

They spent the next two hours smoking more meat. By the time they were done, they had enough for at least two more days. Pierce didn't want to risk trying to keep it any longer. And, if they were lucky, they'd be out of here by then.

"We'd better get rid of that thing. It could attract bears or coyotes," Peck said after they had cut what meat they could eat later that day from the carcass.

"Good idea," Pierce agreed. "What do you think we should do with it?"

"Drag it the fuck out of here. What do you think?"

"Then let's get to it," Pierce said and grabbed one of the hind legs.

Peck hesitated for a moment before grabbing the other leg. "I think we should drag it a least a mile away from our camp just in case it does attract a bear or a coyote."

Peck thought he saw movement along the top of the rock ledge as they dragged the deer away from the camp. The first time he wasn't sure. The second time he was. The creature was shadowing them. "That thing's up on the ridge, watching us," he told Chambers. "I've seen it twice."

Chambers, who had his back to the ridge, hadn't seen it. "Is it there now?"

"I think so, but I don't see it. I've only gotten quick glimpses of it. Trade legs with me and see if you see it."

Once they had switched places Peck had his back to the ridge and Chambers was facing it. They had only gone another ten yards when he stopped and stared at the top of the ridge. "It's still up there. I just saw it moving through the trees."

"What do you think it wants?" Peck asked.

"I don't know, but it's keeping an eye on us. I think this is far enough, let's get rid of this thing and get back to the camp."

Peck nodded and dropped the leg he had been holding.

On the walk back they saw the creature at least three more times. Twice it was nothing more that quick glimpses of it through the trees, but the third time was different. It stood in the open staring down at them, making no move to hide.

Peck stopped and stared at the ridge. "It's up there now," he said, nodding at the spot where the creature stood looking down at them.

When Chambers looked up, the thing glared at them before turning and disappearing back into the trees. Neither of them said anything, they just stood there in stunned silence. It was Chambers who finally broke the spell. "Shit," he cursed under his breath and started walking again. Peck stayed where he was and watched him go.

I've got to find some way to get out of here. Chambers may be content to sit and see what this thing wants, but not me.

Chambers turned and looked back at him when he realized he wasn't following him. "You coming?"

"In a minute, I need to take a … I need some privacy. I'll catch up when I'm done."

"You want me to wait?" Chambers asked.

"No, go ahead. I'll be okay."

"Suit yourself. I'll meet you back there," Chambers answered before continuing his trek back to camp.

Peck watched the ridge where the creature had been to see if it had returned. It hadn't. *Follow him, you prick*, he thought as he waited for Chambers to get out of sight. As soon as he was, Peck turned and ran the other way. He hadn't managed to get more than twenty yards when a roar from the ridge stopped him. He didn't have to look up there to know the creature was staring down at him.

Fuck, he thought and dropped to his hands and knees and started pawing through the dead leaves on the ground as if he was searching for something. When he found a small stone he stood, put it in his pocket and headed back to the camp.

Chambers wasn't there when he arrived. The bow and arrows were also gone. *The prick's running. He left me here as bait for the beast.* He considered running too, until he looked up and saw movement on the ridge. Instead, he ducked under the tarp where he couldn't see it and it couldn't see him. *I hope the damn thing runs him down and crushes his skull like it did the deer. It would serve him right for leaving me here.*

He was still imagining what he wished the monster would do when Chambers came back to camp carrying a pot full of water. "I'm going to make soup. All we've got is the venison, but I thought it would be nice to have some broth with it."

Instead of feeling embarrassed for what he had been thinking, Chambers' arrival only served to piss Peck off even more.

Laura Hickman looked at the Caller ID on her phone's screen and breathed a sigh of relief. It was Jeff Gibbs returning her call. "Jeff, thanks for getting back to me. Are you in town?"

"No, I'm down in Bangor. Why?"

"There's a young man camping out at Pomoola Lake. He's out there on some kind of a dare."

"What?"

"You heard me. You can check it out on his friend's FB page. He's even got a blog. I'll give you the name of the website. You can look it up."

"All right, I'll check it out. What do you want me to do?"

"I want you to go and get the young fool. His girlfriend is up here. She's worried about him and I'm afraid she'll try and get out there by herself to bring him back."

"Shit. Alright, I'll be back tomorrow. Put her off until then."

"All right, I'll talk to her."

Laura cut the connection with Gibbs and immediately dialed Katie's number.

"Hello, Katie? This is Laura Hickman from the Bigfoot Museum," she announced when the girl answered. "I talked to Jeff Gibbs. He's down in Bangor today but he'll be back tomorrow. He's agreed to go out to the lake to look for your friend. How's that sound to you?"

There was a moment's pause before the girl answered. "Tomorrow? There's no way I can get out there today?"

"Not unless you want to walk, and I wouldn't advise that. It's too far and quite easy to get lost. Jeff has an ATV and he knows the way."

"Okay, but I want to go with him."

"I don't know if that's a good idea. It'll be quicker if he goes alone."

"Pierce may think it's some trick of Peck's if this Gibbs guy shows up alone. No, I need to go with him."

There was a slight hesitation before Laura replied. "All right. Just be here tomorrow at noon and he'll take you."

"Fine," the girl answered, but she didn't sound happy about it.

DAY 11

Pierce woke at his usual time just after sunrise. Peck was asleep next to the fire, which had gone out during the night. He had the Bigfoot costume draped over his upper body as a makeshift blanket. Pierce was tempted to wake the asshole up, but then he'd have to deal with him. Better to just let him sleep.

He got quietly dressed, grabbed the pot and was just leaving for the lake when Peck rolled over and demanded, "Where are you going?"

"To take a leak and get some water from the lake. I won't be long."

Peck looked from him to his sleeping nook where the bow and arrows were. Pierce could almost see his thoughts. "If you want to take the bow and leave, go ahead. I don't think you'll make it."

He almost thought Peck might try it, but he didn't. Instead he got up and said, "Wait, I'll go with you?"

Pierce nodded, "Get the bow and arrows and the axe then. I don't think we should leave them here while we're gone."

Peck scrambled to get them. "I think I should take the bow. I'm probably a better shot. You can keep the axe," Pierce told him when he joined him.

"What makes you think you're a better shot?" Peck demanded.

"I've been shooting since I was a kid. I saw it on the Olympics and wanted to try it. I've been shooting ever since."

Peck reluctantly handed them over.

The walk to the lake was uneventful, the walk back not so much. Pierce was looking at the ground ahead of him to avoid the tree roots poking out of the forest floor when Peck suddenly stopped and grabbed him by the arm. "Up there," he hissed.

The creature was glaring down at them from the ledge overlooking the camp. It was only there for a minute, but that was enough to let them know it was watching them.

Pierce stared at the spot where it had been for a minute before continuing back to the campsite. Peck stood frozen where he was. "What the hell does it want?" he asked, his voice cracking in fear.

"What the hell do you think it wants? It wants us. I just don't know why," Pierce answered.

"What are we going to do? We can't just sit here and wait for it to come and get us."

"We're not. We're going to plan and we're going to make some weapons."

"What kind of weapons?"

"Spears, stakes, clubs, anything we can make. We'll do it under the tarp so it can't see what we're doing."

"Will it let us?"

"I don't know … but we have to try."

"We should eat some of the venison and some of the rice," Pierce said when they got back to the camp.

"Right," Peck agreed, but looked as nervous as a kid trying to steal his first candy bar.

Once they had a fire started, Pierce hung the water above the flames. He added a handful of rice once it was boiling. "I'll eat out of the pot, you can have the lid for a plate," he told Peck. "And I only have the one spoon. You're going to have to use your fingers."

When the rice was done, Pierce spooned Peck's share onto the lid and handed it to him.

Peck didn't thank him, he just took it and started eating. When he had finished it, he reached out for another strip of venison. "Better not," Chambers told him. "We should save some for later."

"I'm still hungry," Peck complained.

"Get used to it. I've been hungry since I got here."

Just before sunset the deer they had dragged away from the camp landed with a thump outside the tarp. Peck jumped at the noise and then started shaking when he saw what it was. "What the hell is it doing?"

"I don't think it knows the meat will spoil. It brought it back for us to eat."

"We can't," Peck answered.

"We know that, but it doesn't," Pierce told him. When he stepped out from under the tarp a deep grunt from above told him the creature was there. When he looked up, it pointed at the deer and pantomimed eating.

Pierce shook his head no, then pantomimed eating, throwing up and collapsing on the ground.

"What the hell was that all about?" Peck demanded when Pierce came back to the fire.

Pierce pointed to the dead deer and mimicked what the creature had done. "It made it pretty clear it wanted me to eat the deer. I tried to show it I would get sick if I did."

"Did it understand?"

"I don't know, but it's gone. I guess we'll have to wait and see."

"Are we just going to leave it there and let it attract bears or coyotes?"

Peck and Chambers sat as far apart as they could and still be near enough the fire to stare into its flames and feel its heat. Neither one seemed to want to talk. It was Peck who finally broke the silence. "You want to know why I hate you, Chambers?"

"Yeah, Mike, why?"

"Because everything always comes so easy for you. You're tall, good-looking, can get all the girls you want. You don't have to work for anything. You think you're so superior to guys like me. I could never get a girl like the one who came up here with you. She'd laugh in my face if I asked her for a date."

"You don't know anything about me, Peck. And you never tried to find out."

"Right, and you would have been my best bud if I did, right?"

"Probably not, but we didn't have to be enemies. I never hated you."

"Hah, of course you didn't. It's hard to hate someone you ignore."

"I didn't ignore you, I just avoided you because every time I saw you I could tell you didn't like me and I didn't want to get into an argument with you. I hate confrontations. And, as far as girls go, did you ever see me with one at school?"

"Yeah, last year. You were with that cheerleader. What was her name?"

"Christy, but she was just a study partner. How about any others?"

Peck thought about it for a minute and then had to admit he hadn't.

"That's because I've been going with Katie since high school. I never had much time for sports or parties. I had to spend all my time studying just to pass my classes."

"Oh, bullshit. I never saw you studying."

"That's because I studied in the library. I don't think I ever saw you there."

"Yeah, well I never go there."

"Right, because you don't have to, do you? You're one of those guys who can score good grades without cracking a book. I envied you for that."

"You envied me? That's a laugh."

"Why?"

"Because guys like you don't envy guys like me. We're just a bunch of losers to you. That's why I sent you out here. I wanted you to be the loser for once."

"You know Peck, you're an asshole. It's useless talking to you. Once we're out of here I don't ever want to see you again."

"If we get out of here," Peck answered and tossed a stick into the fire.

Katie was already on her third cup of coffee and staring at the plate of bacon, eggs and home fries sitting on the table in front of her, but was too nervous to eat. She was pushing the eggs around the plate with her fork when her stomach rumbled.

"Alright, I'll eat," she told it, and forced herself to take a mouthful of the cooling eggs.

The waitress stopped at her table with a half full coffee pot. "You okay?" she asked as she reached to refill Katie's cup.

"Yeah, just nervous. I'm going to try and find my boyfriend today. Some guy named Jeff Gibbs is going to take me out to the lake where he's camping."

"Jeff's a good guy. Tell him I said hi when you see him."

"I will," Katie replied, glad to hear the recommendation.

When she was done eating, it was still too early to meet Gibbs, but she drove over to the Bigfoot Museum to wait for him. She wanted to be there if the man showed up early. She was disappointed, but not surprised, to find he wasn't there. When he finally arrived just before noon, she had been sitting in her car for over two hours imagining all sorts of dire things. When a pickup with an ATV on a trailer pulled up she was out of her car and waiting for it before it even came to a stop.

Gibbs got out and approached her. He appeared to be in his forties, and despite his age, he moved with a natural grace and looked to be in good shape. He was an inch shorter than her and streaks of gray were starting to pepper his hair. He had the weathered skin of a man who spends most of his time outdoors.

"Mr. Gibbs? I'm Katie Peters. Ms. Hickman said you can take me to find my boyfriend."

Gibbs stepped back and smiled. "Whoa, slow down. I'll take you out there, but we have to talk first."

"Can't we do that on the way? I'm worried about him."

"Okay, but I need to stop and get a few things on the way over."

"What things?"

"A case of water and a bunch of snacks. Laura told me he's been out there living off the land. If we find him ..."

"When we find him," Katie corrected.

"When we find him, he might need those. Unless you've already thought of that."

"Ah, no. I only thought about getting out there and finding him."

"Don't worry, we will. Hop in and we'll be on our way."

"How long will it take to get there?" was the first thing Katie asked after they were in the pickup.

"Not long, fifteen … twenty minutes."

She was confused until she realized he was referring to the logging road. "No, I mean how long will it take from where Peck dropped him off to the lake where he left him?"

"That depends on the trail. But it will be at least an hour with the ATV."

"How long would it take to walk?"

"Three … maybe four hours. More if you're carrying a backpack full of stuff."

When they arrived at the convenience store, Gibbs sent Katie in to get water and snacks while he filled the ATV's gas tank and a spare five gallon can he had in the pickup's bed. He was just putting the hose back when she came out of the store carrying two large plastic bags. One was filled with bottled water, the other with food.

"What have you got there?" Gibbs asked when she placed them on the floor in front of her.

"Water, sandwiches, beef jerky and a bunch of candy bars."

Gibbs nodded but didn't say anything. Then he started the pickup, pulled back onto the road and they were on their way again. Katie got the impression he didn't want to talk, so she refrained from asking any more questions.

When they finally got to the old logging road, a pickup was already parked in front of the fence with the No Trespassing sign. "That's Peck's truck, the asshole who set all of this up."

"Is that him?" Gibbs asked.

"No, it's a friend of his. He says Peck is out there at another campsite just in case Pierce needs help. That's bullshit though. Peck's out there so he can screw with Pierce. I'm sure of it."

Katie could see Stanley watching in the rearview and side mirrors when she got out of the pickup. When he made no attempt to get out, she walked up and tapped on his window. "Where's your buddy," she demanded when the window went down.

Stanley checked the time on his cell phone before answering. "He's coming," he told her, but he sounded nervous.

Katie saw the look on his face and heard the worry in his voice. "What time was he supposed to be here?"

"Noon."

Katie went back to where Gibbs was unloading the ATV from its trailer. "That guy says Peck was supposed to be here at noon. It's twelve thirty now. Should we wait for him or head in now?"

Gibbs cast a nervous look toward the old road before answering. "Let's give him a few minutes. If he's not here by a quarter-of, we'll head in.

"Didn't you see the No Trespassing sign when you dropped your boyfriend off?" Gibbs asked while they were waiting.

"It wasn't there when I dropped him off. Peck, or his friend over there, must have taken it down because it was there when I came back."

"Really?" Gibbs asked, and went over to look at the sign. Sure enough, the old rusted screws that had fastened it to the fence had been replaced by bright, shiny new ones. Gibbs found that the sign wasn't the only thing Peck had done. The lock was hanging in its place, but the shackle had been cut. Stanley, who had been watching his every move, glanced away when Gibbs turned his gaze to him.

Katie watched as Gibbs took a case from behind the seat of his pickup. "Get your stuff and let's go. Put it in there," he told her, pointing to a metal box attached to a rack behind the ATV's seat. She had to move a coil of rope and a large flashlight out of the way to make room for them. After she had placed her bags in the box, Gibbs placed the case inside and closed the lid. Then he removed the broken lock, dropped it on the ground and opened the gate.

"Climb on," he told Katie. "It may get bumpy in places, so you'll have to hang on."

After she was in the seat next to him, she realized they were lacking another seat. "Where's Pierce going to sit?"

"Where you are. You'll have to sit on his lap."

Jeff Gibbs had been hoping for the best, but doubted that was going to happen. There could be a hundred reasons the Peck kid was late, and he hoped it had something to with the ATV. His fear was that it didn't.

"Keep your eyes open for any sign of them. I'm going to be busy watching the trail. I could miss them," he told Katie over the sound of the engine.

"Okay," she answered.

In places, he could see where the weeds growing in the old road had been beaten down by the passage of Peck's ATV. In others, where the ground was soft, tire tracks were plainly visible. "We're on the right track. I can see someone's been through here recently. We're going to be passing some side trails along the way. If I see that any of them have been used we'll check them out. I wouldn't want to pass right by him."

The ride was uneventful until they came to a side trail that had obviously been used by someone in an ATV. The ground was chewed up from where the wheels had dug in on a slight incline. Gibbs slowed and then stopped when he reached it.

"Why are we stopping?" Katie asked him.

"One set of tracks branches off here. It looks like it's been used more than the main road. I'm going to check it out. Maybe one of them is up there."

"Okay," Katie agreed. "If it's Pierce we can get him and leave. If it's Peck he'll know where Pierce is."

"Keep your eyes open," Gibbs reminded her as he turned onto the side trail.

They had only gone a short way when the remains of Peck's camp came into view.

"Oh, my God!" Katie gasped when she saw it. She was off the back of the ATV and running toward the wreckage before Gibbs could stop her.

"Wait!" he called, but she ignored him. Instead of following her, he went around to the back of the ATV, opened the box that was strapped on the carrier, and took out the case he had put in earlier. From it, he took a gas-fired pistol. It was already loaded with a tranquilizer dart. All he had to do was take the protective tip off to expose the needle and it was ready to go.

When Gibbs reached her, Katie was pouring over the wreckage of the campsite. Any sense of calm she had had up until this point had evaporated. "What happened here? Who could have done this?" she demanded. Then she noticed the pistol. "What's that for?"

"It's a tranquilizer. This," he said, sweeping his arm over the site, "looks like a bear attack."

"A bear? Why would a bear do this?"

"Looking for food. See that cooler over there? It's been torn apart. Bears can destroy a cabin looking for food. A tent would be nothing to them. Hopefully, whoever was camping here was gone when this happened. I don't see any blood, so that's a good thing."

"It's not Pierce's camp. He didn't have a tent. All he had was a big tarp to make a shelter. This must have been Peck's camp. But where is he now?"

Gibbs didn't look at her. Instead he was scanning the trees for movement. "We didn't pass him on the logging road. He's either further in, or he found another way out. We'll keep looking."

Once he was back on the ATV and Katie was seated behind him, Gibbs passed her the pistol. "Hold this, but keep your finger off the trigger. And don't try to shoot anything with it. Just pass it back to me if I ask you for it."

Once Katie was settled in place, Gibbs retraced their path to the logging road and turned toward the lake. He was barely crawling this time, shifting his gaze from the old road to the surrounding trees. He braked to a stop and shut off the engine when he saw the ATV lying in the ditch along the road.

"What? Why are you stopping" Katie asked. She obviously hadn't seen the ATV.

Gibbs pointed. "There's an ATV off the road up here. Its wheels are in the air so it must have flipped. Wait here while I see if anyone's pinned under it."

"There's no way I'm waiting here. I'm going with you."

"Fine," Gibbs answered, and started the engine. There was no sense walking if she insisted on coming.

He braked to a stop and cut the engine when they reached the overturned ATV. Katie beat him off the seat and was in the ditch alongside the wreck before he could even get out.

"There's no one here, but this thing's been torn apart," she called before standing up and looking at him. "I don't think a bear did this. What the hell's going on?"

"I don't know," he told her, but that was a lie. He had seen the large footprint that she hadn't where the creature had stood when it flipped the ATV into the ditch. "Let's keep looking. They have to be out here somewhere."

After the girl climbed back in next to him, he started the ATV and continued on the road, once again at a snail's pace. He doubted they would see the Pomoola unless it wanted to be seen, but he didn't want to speed down the road and take it by surprise.

"This is it," he announced when they reached the marsh without incident.

There were signs that someone had been walking around on either side of the road. "This one looks like it's been used more, so I guess we ought to try it first.

"Stay where you are," he told her when she started to get off. "I don't think I want to leave the ATV here by itself. We'll stay with it as long as we can."

Gibbs wove the ATV through trees and over rocks and roots, picking his way through the woods. Beside him, the girl hung on to keep from being flipped out.

Peck was sitting on the log he had dragged under cover of the tarp arguing that they had to do something, anything, to escape. "We can't just sit here and wait for that thing to come for us. We need to get out of here."

"Quiet. I think I heard something." Pierce told him.

Peck jumped up, alarmed, peering into the woods. "What, the Bigfoot? Where?"

"No, a motor. Quiet."

Peck stopped moving and they both strained to hear the motor Pierce might have heard. At first they heard nothing, then the sound of a motor being revved broke the silence. It was there for less than a minute and then gone again, but there was no mistaking the sound.

Peck was ready to run out of camp to locate it. "Where's it coming from? We have to get to it before they leave."

"Quiet!" Pierce demanded. "Wait until we can tell where it's coming from."

Wait my ass, I'm getting out of here.

"Fuck that. You go that way." He pointed out of camp away from the old logging road. "I'll go this way," and Peck was off, running toward the road.

When the sound came again it was closer and he knew he was going the right way. A minute later he saw its source, a guy and a girl on an ATV.

"Stop! Turn around! We have to get out of here," he yelled as he ran toward it. Then he saw the flaming red hair. It only took a second to realize who she was ... Chambers' girlfriend.

A second later, she was off the ATV and yelling at him.

"Where's Pierce, you asshole!"

"I don't ..." was all he managed to get out before she punched him in the face.

"Bullshit, I talked to your buddy. I know what you've been doing out here. Now where's Pierce?"

Peck stepped back before answering. Then he turned and pointed to the direction he had just come from. "He's back there. Why don't you go find him? But we're not waiting for you. We need to get out of here now."

"We? Who are you talking about?"

"Me and this guy," he answered, indicating Gibbs.

Gibbs gave him an incredulous look and shook his head. "Forget it pal, I came out here for the lady's boyfriend. I'm not leaving until we find him."

Peck was about to answer when he heard a voice behind him. When he turned to look, Chambers was there and he was carrying the bow and arrows.

"I'm right here, you asshole. You weren't trying to leave without me, were you?"

"No, I ..."

As soon as Katie saw Pierce she brushed past Peck and threw herself into his arms. The force of their collision knocked them both to the ground.

"That's enough," Gibbs told them. "We all need to get out of here."

Peck was about to agree when a deep, guttural growl came from the ridge above them. When he looked up, two of the creatures were standing on the ridge above them. It only took him a second to react. While the others were staring up at the creatures he rushed Gibbs, yanked him off the ATV and took his place on the driver's seat. Once onboard, he twisted the throttle, spun the ATV in a sharp turn, and sped off toward the logging road.

Pierce started to chase after him, but Gibbs stopped him. "Don't bother, he won't get far. Let's get to your camp—we need to talk."

"Were those Bigfoots?" Katie asked Pierce in disbelief.

Pierce squeezed her hand. "Yes. Let's get back to my camp and I'll tell you all about it."

Pierce led the way with Katie walking beside him. Gibbs followed close behind. One of the creatures paced them along the ridge. There was no sign of the second one.

"Get under the tarp—it can't see us there," Pierce told them when they arrived at the campsite.

Once they were all there, Pierce told them everything that had happened, starting with finding the dead deer on his walk. Gibbs listened intently without saying anything until he was done. When he finally spoke up, Pierce was amazed at the first question he asked. "Have you gotten it on film yet?"

"No. Why?"

"What about Peck? Did he get any pictures of them?"

"I don't know. Why are you asking me this?"

Gibbs hesitated before answering. "The Pomoola, that's what they're called here, have been here longer than we have. Those of us who know about them keep that secret. That's why this land is off-limits. There are No Trespassing signs at every entry point. If the rest of the world knew they existed, they'd be captured or killed in an instant. We don't want that to happen, so we protect them."

"So, you know about them. Are they dangerous? Will they let us leave?" Katie asked.

"They can be dangerous. As long as we leave them alone,

they stay here in the deep woods and don't cause any problems. Now? I don't know. Either Pierce or Peck must have done something to piss them off."

Then he turned his attention to Pierce. "Tell me what you've been doing since you got here."

"Mostly just looking for food ... and missing her," Pierce said and squeezed Katie's hand.

"That's nice, but how about a little more detail."

"Okay. I've been foraging for carbs and greens. Things like groundnut and cattails. I've been catching fish, and frogs for their legs. I also shot one snake and ... a duck, with the bow. Oh, and some mushrooms." He thought about telling them one had given him hallucinations but decided against it.

"How about Peck? Do you know what he was doing?"

"Other than coming around here and fucking with me? No."

"Fucking with you? How?"

He started by coming over here at night and playing animal sounds, a bear, a coyote and a bunch of grunts from up there on the ridge. He messed up my camp, twice, and then he showed up in a Bigfoot costume ..."

"He what?" Gibbs interrupted.

"He had a Bigfoot costume. It looked pretty good until I saw the real thing. He was wearing it when the thing herded him down here. I damn near shot him with the bow."

"That's what did it. Pomoola are territorial. If they saw a strange Pomoola in their territory they'd attack and kill it."

"But he took the costume off."

"I guess that didn't matter. To them he was an intruder. I imagine the rest of us are too, since we've been with him."

Katie moved closer to Pierce and gripped his hand. "What are we going to do? How are we going to get out of here?"

"Well, I don't think we should stay here. Is there anywhere else we can go?" he asked Pierce.

"Not that I know of. The rest of this is just woods. That's why I made my camp here. The rock ledge provided some natural shelter and protected my back. I think we should stay here tonight and make some plans before we try to leave. I've got the bow, an axe and my knife, so we have some protection."

"And you have that tranquilizer gun," Katie told him.

"Right," Gibbs agreed. "So, let's talk."

Hope flared in Pierce. He had feared they were stuck here. Maybe they'd be able to get out, back to civilization after all. "You have a tranquilizer gun? We can use that to get out."

"It will help. But it might not be enough. It's a single shot. I have to reload every time I use it. It depends on how many of them we have to face at one time."

"How many of them are there?" Katie asked.

"I don't know." Gibbs answered. "We've already seen two. I would imagine there are more."

Pierce was quiet, but Katie spoke up. "But we have to try. We can't just stay here and hope they leave us alone. Can we?"

Gibbs thought for a minute before answering. "Maybe. With Peck gone, who knows? At a minimum, we need to stay here tonight. It's a long walk back. We'd never make it before dark."

"I agree. Katie can sleep up there under the ledge with me, and you can sleep down here near the fire. We should keep it going all night. Maybe it'll keep them away. They've never come near it before."

"I guess that's all we can do," Gibbs agreed.

They were all quiet for several minutes, lost in their individual thoughts. Katie was the first to break the silence. "I wish we hadn't lost the food and water. I'm hungry and thirsty."

"That, I can do something about," Pierce answered. "I have some venison left along with rice and beef jerky. We can get water from the lake. Let me get a fire going and I'll go get some."

"Okay, but we'll all go. It's safer that way," Gibbs told him.

They made their way to the lake with Pierce in the lead with the bow. Katie followed him with the pot and Gibbs acted as rear guard with the tranquilizer.

After filling the pot with water, they headed back to the campsite. Pierce stopped them when it came into view. Katie almost bumped into his back.

"Why are you stopping?"

"I'm looking to see any of the creatures are up on the ridge. This is where we would see them if they were."

They all searched the ridge with their eyes without seeing a Pomoola. "Okay, let's go," Pierce finally told them when he was fairly sure the ridge was clear.

"I have enough venison and rice for tonight and tomorrow morning. We should save the jerky for the hike back tomorrow."

"Good idea," Gibbs agreed.

"I don't have any plates or silverware, so we're going to have to improvise," Pierce told them when the rice was done. "Katie can have the spoon and use the pot's lid as a plate. Jeff, I guess you and I will have to use our fingers and eat out of the pot if you're okay with that."

"Works for me. Let's eat."

When they were done it was still an hour from sunset, but no one wanted to venture away from the perceived safety of the campsite. Katie and Pierce sat next to each other on the ground. Gibbs sat on Pierce's log seat.

"Tell us about these things. These Pomoola," Pierce said.

"The Pomoola have been in this area since before the white man came here. The Abenaki, the local Indians, they have legends about them. We, some of us around here, have known about them for a long time. We keep outsiders out. Back in the twenties it got nasty. Somebody shot one of them, no one knows who, and they killed a couple of hunters. Since then we've left them alone and they've done the same for us. And now you and Peck have managed to upset the apple cart."

"Well, you can kiss those days goodbye once Peck gets back to civilization. He'll be online telling everyone all about them. He'll make shit up if he has to, to get attention."

"Did he get any pictures of them?" Gibbs asked.

"I … don't think so. At least not while he was here."

"Well, that's good anyway."

"Wait a minute," Katie broke in. "We want him to get out, right? If he does he'll send help and we can get out too."

"Maybe," Pierce said. "Knowing him and how much he hates me, he just might take off. He'd never want to admit he just left us here."

"No, but he might want to play the hero."

Pierce thought about that for a minute and then had to agree.

Peck would love to play the hero. He could say the reason he left us here was to get help. "Yeah, he'd probably go online and pull a Kellyanne Conway and fill his posts with a ton of bullshit alternate facts."

When the sun finally set, and the shadows that had filled the woods turned to full dark, Gibbs fed the fire. Within minutes its light filled the space under the tarp and even reached out past its fringes. "You two get some sleep. I'll take the first watch. I'll wake you when I get tired. We'll leave in the morning. We've got a long walk ahead of us."

"Good idea," Pierce agreed, and led Katie to the overhang.

"You sleep on the inside. I'll take the outside," he told her when they climbed into the alcove. That way he would be placing himself between her and the woods.

Katie lay down facing the wall so they could spoon, but quickly rolled over to face out. "I can't sleep facing the wall. I need to see what's happening. Why don't you take the inside so you can hold me and we can both see the woods?"

Pierce wasn't happy about it, but he agreed.

"This sucks," he told her once they were lying together on the remains of his sleeping bag. "I wished you were here every night. Now that you are, I wish you had never come. I want you at home, safe in your own bed."

"I'm not. I'm glad I came. We'll get out of this together. You have to believe that. I do."

Katie had already fallen asleep and Pierce was just dozing off when something sailed off the ledge and hit the ground next to the tarp in the same place the deer had landed.

Oh, shit, Pierce thought, *the deer is back.*

When Peck saw his chance to grab the ATV he didn't think, he just acted. Here was a chance to get the hell out of here and he was taking it. It wasn't until he was back on the old logging road that he slowed down and thought about what he had just done. For one brief second he thought about going back, but his fear of the creatures drove him onward. Once he got out he could call the cops and tell them about the beasts. They could come and get the others out. He told himself that was definitely the best thing to do as the pointed the ATV toward town and hit the gas.

Oh, shit. Is that one of them up ahead? It is, he thought and slowed the ATV to a stop. *Jesus, it looks like a tree standing in the road. Well, there's no turning back. I'll run the fucking thing over if I have to, but I'm getting out of here.* Throwing caution to the wind, he spun the throttle and gunned the ATV toward the creature standing between him and freedom.

It was a bumpy ride, but he was an experienced rider. By the time he reached the Bigfoot, he was going forty miles an hour. It reached out to grab him, but he swerved away from it and ducked low in the seat. He felt its fingers grab his shirt and thought it had him. Then the material ripped and he was past it and in the clear. "Fuck you," he yelled back at it. When he was a hundred yards away he slowed down and looked over his shoulder. The monster hadn't moved. It was standing in the road staring at him. He flipped it the bird before turning back around. Just as he twisted the throttle, a huge hand grabbed him by the arm and ripped him off his seat. Pain lanced through him and he watched in horror as the ATV sped off without him. It only went a few yards before running off the trail.

"No! No! Let me go!" he screamed. The answer was a guttural grunt. In a desperate effort to free himself, he kicked at the Bigfoot's groin and swung at its face with his free hand. The monster growled in anger and shook him so hard it snapped the bones in the arm it was holding. Peck screamed in pain as pieces of bone ripped through his skin. Then it tossed him over its shoulder and carried him like a big man might carry a child. When he tried to struggle, the beast shook him so hard Peck passed out.

Peck groaned as he slowly returned to consciousness. His vision was blurred, but he could smell the musky odor of the beast that was carrying him. It must have sensed he was awake because it threw him to the ground with bone-jarring force. Pain lanced through his broken arm and he passed out again.

The next time he woke he was facing two of the creatures. One was smaller and obviously female. If he thought she might be any gentler than the male, he was sadly mistaken. When she saw he was awake, she rushed over and rammed her face against his. She bit him when he opened his mouth to scream. The wicked canines sank into his cheeks. Then she squeezed her jaws shut and ripped her head back, tearing away half of his face.

Stanley sat in the pickup and watched the man and girl drive off down the old logging road toward Peck and Chambers.

Mike's screwed. He's going to meet them on the road and Chambers' girl is going to let him have it. When she gets back she's going to go online and tear him ... us ... a new asshole. We ought to pack up our stuff and get the hell out of here. If he gets online first he might be able to spin it his way.

Three hours later, when Peck still hadn't arrived, Stanley was torn between leaving and staying. He checked his phone for what must have been the hundredth time hoping that he had a least one bar. And, like each previous time, it showed that there was no service.

When the sun finally started to set, he decided that Peck wasn't coming. *I'll go back to the room and come back in the morning. If he does come back tonight, he can always drive the ATV to the motel.*

Pierce was trying to decide what to do about the deer when Gibbs whispered just loud enough for him hear, "Chambers, you'd better get down here."

He tried to get up without waking Katie, but she woke as he stood up. "What?" she asked, and he could hear the concern in her voice.

"You remember the deer I told you about? I think it's back. Stay here and I'll check."

"The hell with that. I'm coming."

"Is it the old deer, or a new one?" he asked Gibbs once he was under the tarp.

"Neither. It's Peck."

Day 12

Peck's body was lying face down just outside the cover of the tarp. White bone fragments poked through the skin of his broken arm. One of his legs was twisted at an impossible angle.

"That's Peck alright. Those are my clothes he's wearing," Pierce told them.

"What are we going to do with him," Katie asked.

Pierce looked from her to Gibbs. "I don't know. What can we do with him?"

Gibbs finally said what they were all thinking. "There's nothing we can do with him. We have to leave him here. We can't bury him, we don't have anything to dig with. And, we sure can't carry him out."

"But ..." Katie started to say and then fell silent. Peck was an asshole, but even he didn't deserve to be left out here in the woods to be eaten by animals. But Gibbs was right, they had to look out for themselves.

"If we're going to leave him, we should do it," she finally said. "He's creeping me out. I don't want to have to see him anymore."

"We should eat first, and drink some water. It's going to be a long, dry walk back to the road where my pickup is parked." Gibbs told her.

"How can I eat after seeing that?"

"You have too. We can't carry the food, and it's a long walk. I've still got enough venison for breakfast. We can have it along with some rice. We'll save the jerky for the walk back. Before we leave we can fill the pot with water and take it with us," Pierce told them.

Katie sat with her back to Peck while they were eating, but

that didn't keep her from thinking about him. She had never been that close to a dead body before. Hell, she had never even been to a funeral. "I keep imagining he's going to suddenly jump up and accuse me of getting him killed. It know it's ridiculous, but I can't stop thinking about it."

Pierce took her hands in his and gave them a gentle squeeze. "Would it help if I covered him with something?"

"No, let's just do what we have to do and get out of here."

When they were ready to go, Pierce strung the bow. "Only use that if you have to. Let me use this first if I can," Gibbs said, holding up the tranquilizer pistol.

"Okay, but if one of them gets near her I'll kill if I can," Pierce answered, nodding at Katie.

It was too difficult to walk with an arrow nocked and ready to use. Instead, Pierce walked with the bow strung and a hunting arrow in his other hand. That was the best he could do. He found himself continually glancing up at the ridge to see if they were being shadowed by the Pomoolas.

"Have you seen any?" Katie finally asked.

"No, but that doesn't mean they aren't up there. I think we only see them when they want us to."

"Exactly," Gibbs agreed. "Once we get on the old logging road we'll have a better chance. It's more open. We may never see them. They may just let us go."

"Do you really think so?" Katie asked, a note of hope in her voice.

"I don't know. I hope so, but with Pomoola, you can never tell. Just keep looking."

When they reached the road, Pierce felt some of the tension ease from his neck and shoulders. Here at least they had the marsh at their backs and a good view all around. "Let's take a break before we head out," he suggested.

"Okay, but not too long." Gibbs agreed. "We've got a long way to go."

Their "break" only lasted a few minutes before Pierce started fidgeting. "I can't just sit here like this. It's driving me crazy. Let's go."

After a few minutes, Pierce started talking just to break the silence. "See that? That's hopniss. I've eaten it a couple of times."

"I remember that. What else is it called?" Katie asked.

"Groundnut. It'll never replace potatoes, but it's not bad."

They had only been walking for ten minutes when Katie suddenly stopped. Gibbs almost ran into her from behind. "What?" he asked, scanning the woods.

"Something moved in there among the trees. I'm not sure what it was, but it was big."

"Could it have been a deer, or a moose?" Pierce asked. He had already nocked a hunting arrow and was scanning the trees where Katie said she had seen the movement.

"Well, whatever it was, it's gone or hiding. We should keep moving," Gibbs told them.

The walk was uneventful until Pierce saw wheels poking up from the side of the road. "There's an ATV off the road up here. It's upside down."

Gibbs walked up beside him. "That's Peck's. We saw it on our way in, but we didn't search it. We should see if there's anything we could use."

They were about to give up when Katie found the Bigfoot mask that the Pomoola had torn in two. It was lying in the grass in two pieces. She picked one up in each hand and held them out for Pierce and Gibbs. "What the hell is this?"

Gibbs frowned and shook his head when he saw them. "That's the reason they came after him. If he came walking up the road carrying that in one hand it would look like he had killed one of them."

"He was wearing the rest of the costume when he came running down the road," Pierce told him.

"I don't think that would have mattered. Not at that point. When you took him to your camp, they probably associated you with him. Same thing with us."

Katie threw the pieces down in disgust. "Well, there's nothing here for us. We might as well keep walking."

"Peck's camp is off that way," Gibbs told Pierce when they came to a branching road that showed a lot of use. "He had quite a setup until the Pomoolas tore it apart."

"Is there anything there we can use?" Katie asked.

"I don't think so. It's better to just keep walking."

"Right," Pierce answered and once again took the lead. They had only gone a few hundred yards when he saw the back of Gibbs' ATV. "Here's your ATV," he announced, and ran toward it, a flare of hope blossoming in his head. It was still upright, but wasn't in much better shape than Peck's. The seats were shredded and all the wires had been torn off the engine.

"We're not using that to get out," he told them, disappointment obvious in his voice. "Let's keep going."

They started to do just that when Gibbs stopped them. "Let's check the box first. That doesn't look damaged."

When he undid the latches, the contents had been untouched. "Well, we've got food and water anyway. That's helpful. We should eat the sandwiches now and take what water we can carry."

He handed the plastic bag with the sandwiches to Pierce, whose mouth actually watered as he ripped the clear plastic wrap from one of them. He took a cautionary sniff, didn't find anything that smelled bad, so he took a huge bite out of it. He wanted to savor it, roll it around in his mouth, but it was impossible. He swallowed and took a second bite before he was able to control himself.

"Hey, slow down. It's not going anywhere," Katie said, laughing at him.

"Sorry. It's just that I haven't had anything I didn't catch or forage for since I've been here. I've dreamed of this."

"What? You didn't dream of me?"

"Of course I did. But I can't eat ..." he started to say, and then almost choked on the last bite and turned red.

"Never mind," she said, and handed him an open bottle of water. He had just taken the first sip when a loud howl broke the silence. It was answered by a second, and then a third. Then, hardly audible, off in the distance, a fourth.

"Damn, we'll never be able to handle four of them. We need to go, now! Don't run, walk," Gibbs said, and started walking fast up the road. He hadn't gone more than ten yards when two of the Pomoola appeared on the road in front of him. They were out of range of the tranquilizer gun, but it was a single shot anyway.

"Do you want me to shoot it?" Pierce asked, nocking an arrow.

"Christ, no! Put that thing down. We need to go back to your camp. We can defend that if we have to. We're too out in the open here."

Pierce thought about it. He was tempted to take the shot regardless of what Gibbs said. If Katie hadn't been with them he might have done it, but he wasn't willing to risk it with her there. "All right, let's go," he finally answered. "But let's take the water and food with us."

"Good idea," Gibbs agreed, and they took what they could carry.

Pierce tried to ignore the creatures, but it was impossible. Every time he turned to look back, one of them was following. As disturbing at that was, it was the ones he couldn't see that bothered him the most.

Katie walked between Pierce and Gibbs. She stared straight ahead, refusing to turn and look back up the road. Every time Pierce glanced back, she could tell by the look on his face that the creatures were still there. She wanted to yell, *Stop looking at them*, but couldn't bring herself to do it. Once they reached the marsh, she chanced a glance back before stepping off the road to head toward Pierce's campsite. A single Pomoola seemed to fill the road behind them. She gasped in terror. It was her first good look at the thing. It appeared to be much larger and more menacing that the one she had seen in the museum.

"Try not to look at it," Gibbs said when he saw her face.

She tore her gaze away when she realized she was staring at it. "Where's the other one?"

"Don't know. I haven't seen it," Pierce answered. "How about you, Gibbs?"

"No, and why don't you call me Jeff? It looks like we might be stuck with each other for a while."

"Okay, Jeff," Pierce agreed, and led them back to his camp.

Katie dreaded going back. She did not want to see Peck's

body. She had managed to put it out of her mind on the way out. Now she was faced with having to see it again. That was the last thing she wanted to do, so she avoided looking over where the corpse was when they got back to the campsite. She was about to ask Pierce and Gibbs to cover Peck with something when she heard Pierce say, "What the hell, he's gone."

She was relieved until she understood what it meant. The Pomoolas must have come and taken him. Either that, or a bear. Both possibilities were terrifying. Even though she knew they wouldn't have an answer, she had to ask, "What happened to him?"

It was Gibbs who answered, "It must have been the Pomoolas. It looks like nothing else has been touched. A bear would have torn everything apart."

"But why would they take his body?" Then one reason occurred to her and she turned and vomited into the woods.

Pierce went to her and put his hand on her shoulder as she stood doubled over. "What?"

"What use could they have for a dead body except to eat it? That's why they threw the deer down here. Are they keeping us here as a handy source of food? We know they eat meat. You said that yourself."

"No. Of course not," he answered, but she could tell he wasn't sure. Then he turned to Gibbs. "What about it, Jeff. Would these things eat Peck?"

Gibbs hesitated before answering. "I honestly don't know. I've never heard of them doing that."

"But?" Katie asked.

"But … people used to disappear around here. No one knows what happened to them. That's why I agreed to come out here and get Pierce. I would have come by myself if you hadn't insisted on coming with me. I was going to tell Peck to leave too."

"What about Ms. Hickman? She knows you're out here, doesn't she? Will she send someone else when you don't come back?"

"Who's Ms. Hickman?" Pierce asked.

"Laura Hickman. She runs the Bigfoot Museum in town."

Gibbs answered. "Yes, she'll probably get in touch with the local game warden, Joe Blaizdell. But that won't be for a day or two. She'll wait, hoping we'll come, back before she does that."

"So we just have to stay put for a couple of days and someone should be coming? We should be able to do that, shouldn't we?" Pierce asked.

"Yeah, but we have to make some plans."

"What have you got in mind?"

"We all stick together. No one goes off alone."

"What if I have to go to the bathroom?" Katie asked. "I'm not doing that with you two watching."

"I understand," Gibbs answered. "But you can't go alone. Pierce can go with you as long as you don't go far. He doesn't have to hold your hand, but he needs to keep you in sight. Can you live with that?"

Katie frowned and shook her head. "If I have too."

"You do. Either that, or hold it."

Maybe I got the day wrong, Stanley thought when he woke up at the motel. *I'll go back out today and see if Mike's there. If not, I don't know what I'm going to do. I'm sure as hell not going to hike out there, though. It's too damn far.*

Stanley was back at the meeting place the next day at noon. The other pickup and trailer were still there and there was no sign of Peck.

What the hell do I do now? If I call the cops and he's okay, he's going to be pissed. Plus, he might get arrested for trespassing. If he's hurt or something and I don't call the cops, then what? Chambers' girlfriend and that other guy are out there, too. If he's in trouble they can help him. One more day. I'll wait one more day. If he's not back by tomorrow, I'll call someone.

Jeff, Jeff, Jeff. Where the hell are you? What's going on out there?

Laura Hickman was struggling with the same problem Stanley was. The difference was, she knew what was out there and what it could mean. She also knew that calling in the game wardens was not something she wanted to do. If Jeff wasn't back by tomorrow, she'd have no choice.

"What time is it?" Pierce asked, gazing up at the night sky.

Katie took out her phone, turned it on and waited for it to display the time. "Just past midnight."

Gibbs stood, stretched and then placed another piece of wood on the fire. Sparks erupted from it and rose into the night sky as the logs shifted. "I'll take the first watch. You two get some sleep."

Pierce watched as the piece of wood Gibbs added to the fire caught. He didn't think he'd be able to sleep, but he knew both he and Katie needed it. "Okay," he agreed. Then he led Katie to his sleeping space under the overhang.

Peck had torn the sleeping bag apart when he trashed the campsite, but they could still use it as a covering for the moss and leaves he used for a mattress. He lay down on the outside so he could be between her and the woods, leaving room for her on the inside. This time she didn't complain about facing the rock wall. As soon as she lay down beside him, and they were snuggled together like spoons, he knew it wasn't going to work. All he could see was the stone wall in front of them. Shadows from the fire danced across it, igniting wild thoughts in his imagination. When he couldn't take it any longer, he rolled over and faced the woods.

This isn't any better, he thought. Now he could see into the dark, but he couldn't hold her.

"What's the matter?" she asked as she rolled over and snuggled into his back.

"I need to see what's out there."

"Okay, but get behind me. I want you to hold me."

Once he did, and she was back in his arms, he started to relax. "I still wish you weren't here. You know that, right?"

"I know," she told him. "But I'm glad I am."

"Why?"

"Because I love you, you idiot."

DAY 13 – 1

Katie woke, disoriented and alone, under the rock shelf. It took her a minute to realize what she was looking at. Pierce was sitting under the tarp gazing into the fire. Gibbs lay curled up asleep between them. She sat up, stiff from sleeping on the ground, and realized she needed to go to the bathroom.

"I need to pee," she told Pierce when she joined him at the fire.

Pierce stood up, looked at the sleeping Gibbs and nodded. "I'll go with you."

She gave him an incredulous look before saying, "You're not going to watch me pee."

"Well, I'm not letting you go alone. We agreed on that. You can go behind a tree or something, but I want to be able to make sure you're safe. Just let me get the bow and arrows."

She thought about arguing, but she really needed to go, so she waited and tried not to squirm.

This is ridiculous. He's seen me naked, we've made love, and I'm embarrassed to let him see me squat and pee in the woods, she thought as she dropped her shorts and squatted behind an oak tree. When she was done, she used one of the napkins she had brought with the sandwiches to dry off. *What the hell has Pierce been using since he's been out here? They never talk about that on those survival shows.*

After she had pulled her shorts back up, something, some movement on the stone ridge that ran behind the camp caught her eye. She had to stare at it for a minute before she realized one of the creatures was standing there watching her. It blended in so well with its background that she never would have seen it if it hadn't moved.

She blew right by Pierce in her hurry to get back to the campsite and under the tarp. As soon as she was there she sat down on Pierce's log and hugged herself.

"What's wrong?" he asked when he caught up to her.

"One of those things was up on the ridge watching me pee."

"Damn," Pierce swore.

"Did you just see the one?" Gibbs asked, fully awake now.

She looked at him like he was crazy. "Isn't one enough?"

"Of course it is, but it's better than two, or three."

Katie shivered at the thought. "I only saw one, but it blended in so well there could have been more. I only noticed that one because it moved."

"Does it matter? One. Two, three? We're still trapped here," Pierce told him.

"It does matter. If there's just one of them, I could tranq it and we could make a break for it. If there were two or three, it would be a lot harder."

"How do we find out?" Katie asked.

"I don't know. I think we should sit tight for a day and watch. Maybe the damn things will just leave."

"You really think so?"

Gibbs shook his head before answering. "No. But we can hope." Then he turned his attention to Pierce. "How much food do we have?"

"We've got rice, jerky and some of the deer left. Fish are easy to catch if we want that."

Katie had no thoughts of leaving the shelter of the tarp and said so. "No. I want to stay under here where they can't see me. What we have is fine."

Pierce was surprised at how vehemently Katie reacted to the idea of leaving the shelter of the tarp. Eventually he got it though. All the Pomoolas they had seen appeared to be male. She had no idea what they would do now that they had seen her peeing and it was obvious she was a female.

"Okay, we'll stay here, but we should try and find out how many of them are up there."

"How are you going to do that?"

Pierce motioned to the woods. "I'm going to sit out there and watch for them."

When Katie gave him a nervous look, Gibbs spoke up. "Pierce, you stay under here with her. I'll watch for them."

When Pierce agreed, the look of relief on Katie's face was apparent. "Tell me we're going to get out of here," she said, looking around nervously.

"Don't worry. I'm sure we will," he reassured her, but that was not what he was thinking. *Will we get out of here? I'm not so sure. If no one comes for us, we're going to have make a break for it.*

After an hour of sitting around doing nothing, Pierce felt the need to do something... anything, to break the monotony. "Have you seen anything?" he asked Gibbs.

Gibbs nodded. "There's one of them up there. I've seen it off and on since I've been out here. It comes to the edge, looks down here and then fades back into the trees."

"Why didn't you say anything?" Katie demanded.

"What good would it have done? All it could do was make things worse."

"Is it up there now?" Pierce asked.

"I can't see it, but it probably is."

"Next time you see, it tell us. I want to try something."

"What?" Katie demanded.

"Leaving the shelter. Not toward the road, toward the lake. If it lets us, we can try to catch some fish for dinner. If we can get it comfortable with our leaving the campsite it may make it easier for us to leave. Plus, we need water."

"That's probably a good idea," Gibbs agreed. "I'll let you know the next time I see it."

Twenty minutes later Katie was tired of waiting. "Let's just do it. We need to know if it's up there or not."

"Okay," Pierce agreed. "You take the pot for water and I'll bring my fishing line and bow." Even though it was her idea, Katie still hesitated before following him out from under the tarp.

"Don't look back. It's up there," Gibbs told them as he stood up to join them. "It just seemed to materialize out of the trees when you came out."

"What's it doing?"

"Nothing. It's just watching. I'll stay here and keep an eye on it for a few minutes. Then I'll join you at the lake."

"Right," Pierce agreed.

"Damn," Pierce swore when they reached the lake.

"What," Katie asked, looking around in alarm.

"I totally forgot about bait. We're going to have to find some."

He was pawing through a pile of dead leaves when Gibbs joined them. "What are you doing down there?" the man asked when he saw Pierce on his hands and knees on the ground.

"I forgot bait. I'm looking for anything I can use. What happed with the Pomoola?"

"I watched it until you were almost out of site. Then I started to follow you. I heard a thump and turned around. The damn thing jumped off the ridge and followed me here."

Katie looked back at the way they had come and scanned the trees. "Where is it? I don't see it."

"Don't worry, it's back there. Those things can hide in plain sight."

Then, as if to prove his point, the creature appeared as if from nowhere. One second it wasn't there, and the next it was. It glared at them for a minute and then faded back into the woods.

She stared in disbelief before asking, "How are we going to get away from them if we can't even see them?"

"It'll be better once we're on the road. It's more open there." Pierce assured her. "For now, help me find some bait so we can catch dinner."

Finding bait turned out to be more time consuming than catching fish. After a half hour of searching, all Pierce managed to come up with were a few grubs. Gibbs had better luck sorting through a thick pile of damp leaves, uncovering four fat earth worms. While they had been looking for bait, Katie had stood watch for the Pomoola. For what it was worth, she never saw it. In a way, that was more frightening than actually seeing it would have been. It could have been gone, or right there watching them the entire time.

With bait in hand, Pierce landed half a dozen striped perch in a matter of minutes. "That should do it," he told them after he dragged the last one in. "Let's fill the pot with water and head back after I clean these fish."

Katie looked at the slime and dirt in the bottom of the pot and grimaced. "Yuck, what have you got to clean this with?"

"Leaves, dirt and elbow grease. Dish detergent wasn't on my list of ten extra items."

Once the fish were cleaned, Pierce placed the filets in the pot and tossed the rest of the remains in the lake. When Katie gave him a questioning look, he told her, "It seems to attract more fish."

They made their way back to the campsite, Katie carrying the pot full of water and fish, Pierce the bow and fishing line. Gibbs kept an eye out for the Pomoola.

"What about greens. Can we find some of those?" Katie asked.

"Yeah, but we'd have to go out to the old road. I'm not sure that's a good idea, but we could give it a try. I know where there's some groundnut."

"I saw some mushrooms on the way here. We could use those too," Gibbs told him.

Pierce grimaced at the thought of the mushrooms. "I don't know. I had a bad experience with them."

"These will be fine. I know my mushrooms."

"As long as you're *sure*. I thought the ones I ate were okay, but they weren't. They made me sick as hell."

"Don't worry, I pick them every year. I haven't made a mistake yet."

"Fine, as long as you're sure. Then can go get that groundnut."

"What the hell is groundnut?"

"It's a tuber. You'll see."

"Should we bring these?" Katie asked, holding up the pot of fish. "You think they'll be safe there? They won't attract bears or animals, will they?"

"I don't think so. Not with our friends up there."

There was no sign of the Pomoolas on the hike to the marsh. As soon as they stepped out onto the old road, however, one of the creatures emerged from the woods fifty yards from them and took up a position barring them from trying to leave.

"Ignore it," Gibbs whispered. "Let's get what we came for and get back to the camp."

The walk back was also free of Pomoolas, but when they got there, a surprise was waiting for them. Katie was the one who found it. Peck's body was back. But this time it had been ravaged. Half his face was gone and the top of his skull had been torn off. His brain was missing. "Oh, my God," she gasped, and staggered away from it, retching and clutching her stomach.

Pierce was stunned. "Jesus Christ! They ripped his brain out. Why would they do that?"

Gibbs collapsed onto the log Pierce used as a chair. "To eat it. Wild things will eat the brain first if they can."

"Then why throw him down here? Why not keep the rest of him?"

"You ate part of the deer they gave you. Maybe they thought you'd eat him too," Gibbs answered.

"Get rid of him," Katie called out between retches.

Pierce looked at her and nodded his agreement. "Yeah, we have to bury him … or something. Something to let the creatures know we don't eat our dead."

"How? Do you have a shovel, or anything else to dig with?" Gibbs asked.

"No," Pierce admitted. Then, after thinking, "we could load him up with rocks and sink him in the lake."

Katie groaned. "Ugh. You guys do it. I don't want to touch him."

Gibbs looked at Pierce and nodded. "Right. Let's find some rocks. It'll get rid of the body and keep it safe from them."

"We can take them from the fire pit. I can always find more later."

It only took a minute to realize that was a bad idea. There was no way they were going to be able to carry Peck and enough stones to sink him to the bottom in one trip.

"Let's just take him and try and find the stones when we reach the water," Gibbs suggested.

Just before they left, Pierce retrieved Peck's Bigfoot costume from where he had stuffed it under a pile of leaves and firewood.

"What's that for?" Katie asked.

"We'll put it on him and stuff it full of rocks. That way we can get enough weight to hold him down."

After trying unsuccessfully several ways to share the burden of carrying the body, Pierce ended up putting it over his shoulder in a fireman's carry. That worked best, but by the time they reached the lake he was exhausted. "Thank God," he said, as he dumped it on the shore at the edge of a deep drop-off Pierce had found when he was swimming. "Give me a minute and we can look for some stones."

"You rest, we'll find them," Katie told him, and she and Gibbs started hunting along the shore line. While they were gone, Pierce wrestled Peck's corpse into the costume and rolled him over, face down. He didn't want to have to look at his ravaged face.

It took three trips for Katie and Gibbs to gather enough rocks to ensure they had enough to hold Peck's corpse down. After stuffing them into the costume, they rolled him off the ledge and watched him sink into the lake. The dark-colored costume disappeared long before Peck's ravaged face did. The face stared accusingly up at them as it sank to the bottom. Eventually, it also disappeared into the murky depths.

Katie looked at the grilled perch, mushrooms and groundnut that Pierce had piled on the lid of the cooking pot for her. "I don't think I can eat. Not after what we did today,"

"Take it, you have too. If you don't, you'll be starving later. Believe me, I know."

She took it, but reluctantly.

Pierce, Katie and Jeff ate in silence, each lost in their own thoughts. When they were done, Gibbs stirred the fire with a branch. Glowing embers joined the smoke rising into the air. "We should think about getting out of here as soon as possible," he told them and tossed the branch into the flames.

Katie glanced nervously around the woods. "We can't go now, it's too late. We'd never make it before dark."

"Agreed. But tomorrow … we should do it then."

"Why?" Pierce asked. "If we wait, maybe they'll just go

away."

"Do you really want to risk that? What if they attack and carry one of us off?" Gibbs answered, looking directly at Katie.

"Okay. In the morning," Pierce agreed.

When evening came and Gibbs still hadn't returned, Laura Hickman decided she had to call the game warden. It was not a conversation she was looking forward to. She breathed a sigh of relief when Joe Blaizdell's phone rang for the sixth time without him answering. She was about to hang up when he finally picked up.

"Laura, what can I do for you?" Blaizdell said when he came on the line. She was shocked he knew it was her until she realized he must have Caller ID. She still wasn't used to that.

Here goes, she thought, and told him about Jeff Gibbs and the kids camping out on the lake.

"How long has he been gone?"

"Two days. That's too long. He was going to get them and come right back."

"Damn," Blaizdell muttered. "Well, I guess I'm going to have to go get them. I'll take Adam with me. He's got to learn about them sometime."

"Can you trust him?"

"Yeah. He'll be alright."

Now it was Joe Blaizdell's turn to make a call he didn't want to. He dialed the number and was still deciding what to say when the other warden answered. "Adam, this is Joe. I need you to meet me at the Bigfoot Museum in Tinkers Falls tomorrow morning. We need to rescue some kids camping out in the woods. Can you be there at eight?"

"Sure. What's going on?"

"I'll fill you in then. Bring your ATV. You'll need it."

Joe Blaizdell and Laura Hickman were waiting in Blaizdell's pickup when Adam Grant pulled into the museum's parking lot. Blaizdell was pleased to see Grant had brought his ATV as requested.

"What's up?" Grant asked when all three were out of their

vehicles.

"Come inside and I'll fill you in," Blaizdell answered.

Both men followed Laura to the museum where she unlocked the door and led them inside.

"You ever been here before?" Blaizdell asked once they were inside.

Grant looked around the room before answering. "Can't say that I have. I've never had that much of an interest in the Bigfoot legends."

"Well, that's about to change. You might actually get to see one today."

Grant gave him a skeptical look. "You're joking ... right?"

"I wish he was," Laura Hickman answered. "The Bigfoot are real, but around here we call them Pomoola."

"You're telling me, these things," Grant said, nodding at the Bigfoot statue, "are real and living around here?"

"Yep."

Grant shook his head in disbelief. "Blaizdell, you actually believe this stuff?"

"I do, because I've seen them."

Grant walked over to the Bigfoot statue. Even at six-foot, he was dwarfed by it. "These? You've actually seen one of these?"

"I have, and you might get to see one today yourself. Jeff Gibbs and three twenty-somethings are out in the woods where Pomoola live sometimes. Jeff was supposed to go out, get the kids, and come right back. That was two days ago. They never came back. We're going to go out and find out why."

Grant looked up at the face of the statue and shivered. The sheer size of the beast was intimidating. He couldn't imagine meeting one in the woods. "I'll don't believe it, but I'll go along with you until I find out what's really going on."

"That's okay too. Follow me out to where we're going."

When Blaizdell and Grant arrived at the fence blocking the old logging road, Stanley was already parked there in Peck's pickup. Blaizdell got out of his truck and strolled to Stanley's open window. "Morning. Mind if I ask you what you're doing out here?"

Stanley's gaze shifted between him and the No Trespassing sign. When he seemed hesitant to answer, Blaizdell asked him again.

"Waiting for a friend," Stanley finally admitted.

"Someone's cut around the gate," Grant called from where he was looking at the tracks Peck's and Gibbs' ATVs had left in the brush.

Blaizdell gave Stanley a hard glare. Then he asked, "Is that the friend you're waiting for?"

"Yeah," Stanley admitted.

"How long have you been waiting?"

"Ah … about an hour."

"And before that?"

This time Stanley took longer to answer. "Two days. He was supposed to meet me here then, but he never showed up."

"Why didn't you call us?"

Stanley fidgeted, obviously not happy with the way the conversation was going. "I didn't want to get him in trouble," he finally managed to admit.

"Well, it looks like he already is, so I'd advise you to leave."

"Yes, sir," Stanley said. A minute later he started the pickup and drove away.

"Did you get his name?" Grant asked when he joined Blaizdell.

"No"

"Plate number?"

"No."

"Why not?"

"Why would I need it? He wasn't trespassing. Besides, I don't want him hanging around when we get back."

"Okay, it's your show. Let's get the ATVs unloaded and go find those people."

"Before we do that, I need to brief you on what to expect and what to do … and not do."

Grant gave him a skeptical look, but didn't say anything. He just waited for Blaizdell to go on.

"If we see a Pomoola, don't tranq it unless you have no other choice."

"With what? I didn't bring a tranquilizer gun with me."

"That's why I brought one for you. Two, actually … a pistol and a rifle. Plus, I've got two for myself."

"You're serious about this Bigfoot thing, aren't you?"

"You're damn right I am. So keep your eyes out for them. If we see one, don't provoke it. Don't yell or do anything to challenge it. All we want to do is find Gibbs and the three kids and bring them back. Got it?"

"Got it," Grant said, but still sounded doubtful.

Once they had unloaded the ATVs, and Blaizdell had given Grant the tranquilizer guns and darts, he led the way around the gate and up the old logging road.

When Pierce opened his eyes, Gibbs was awake and feeding wood to the fire. The sun was already up, and yellow sunlight filtered through the trees. He was trying to decide what time it was when he remembered Gibbs had a watch.

"Seven thirty," Gibbs answered when Pierce asked.

"Did you stay up all night? You were supposed to wake me to stand watch."

"I figured you guys could use the sleep. Now that you're awake I'll grab a few hours and then we can try to leave."

"What's going on?" Katie asked as she joined them under the tarp.

"Gibbs stayed awake all night so we could sleep. He's going to get a few hours now and then we can head out."

"Wake me at noon. That will give us plenty of time to get back to my truck."

"I've got to pee," Katie said after Gibbs had settled down under the overhang.

"Me too," Pierce told her. "Let's go, but not too far."

This time when Katie got to the oak tree she had ducked behind before, she positioned herself so the trunk was between her and the ridge so the Pomoola couldn't see her. The problem was, now she was in plain sight to Pierce. "Turn around, please," she asked when it appeared he wasn't going to.

"Oh, sorry," he answered, as did as she asked.

When she was done, he traded places with her. Then he

turned his back to her, unzipped and relieved himself. He didn't care if she watched, but there was no need to be gross about it either.

Once they were back under the tarp, Katie glanced up at the overhang. Gibbs had his back to them and appeared to be asleep. "Kiss me," she said and wrapped her arms around Pierces' neck. He did, fiercely and deeply and could feel himself becoming aroused against her. She ground her hips into him before jerking away. "Later," she told him. "After we get out of here."

If we get out of here, he thought, as he released her.

They woke Gibbs exactly at noon. The man was awake and on his feet seconds after Pierce shook his shoulder. Pierce had never seen anyone come out of a sound sleep so quickly.

"Okay, let's do it," he told them.

Before leaving, they went over exactly what they were going to do. Gibbs would take point with the tranquilizer gun, Katie would be in the middle, and Pierce would bring up the rear with the bow. He would only use it if it was absolutely necessary.

On the way to the logging road, Pierce kept glancing from Katie's back to the top of the rock ledge. He never saw any movement there, and by the time they reached the old logging road he entertained hopes that the Pomoolas had given up and left them. Those hopes were shattered when one of the creatures stepped out of the woods when they turned away from the marsh.

"Keep walking. Let's see what it does," Gibbs told them. Then, with Gibbs in the lead, they did just that.

Pierce's heart started racing when the creature raised up to its full height and pointed at them, and then in the direction of their camp.

Gibbs pointed out the obvious. "It wants us to turn around and go back. Let's see what it does if we don't."

When they didn't, it grunted at them and moved down the path toward them, all the while pointing back toward their camp. Its gestures became more agitated the longer they stood their ground and the closer it got to them.

"Shoot it," Katie cried when the distance between them had

dropped to thirty yards.

Gibbs waited until it was twenty yards away before raising the pistol and pulling the trigger. A second later a bit of red fluff blossomed on the creature's chest. The Pomoola glanced down at it before ripping it out and throwing it to the ground, but the damage had already been done. A charge inside the dart had injected the tranquilizer into its body on contact. Then it started coming toward them again.

Pierce couldn't hide his alarm when the dart seemed to have no effect on the monster. "Why is it still coming? Didn't it work?"

"It takes a few minutes. Turn around and start walking back toward the camp," Gibbs answered. As soon as they did that, the Pomoola stood its ground, watching them go. A few minutes later it dropped to one knee, and then pitched forward on its face in the road.

"Now. Let's go," Gibbs told them as soon as it was down.

"How long have we got?" Pierce asked as they hustled past the creature.

"About forty-five minutes. When it wakes up it's going to be groggy, so maybe a little longer until it realizes we're gone."

Katie stopped and stood over the creature. "Why not give it another shot?"

"Because that would kill it. We definitely don't want to do that."

"Why the hell not?" Pierce demanded.

"Because that would really piss the rest of them off. I only have five more darts, and we don't know how many of them there are. Now let's go."

Pierce stopped when they came across Peck's ruined SUV. "That asshole," he muttered under his breath and then felt bad for saying it. Peck *had* been an asshole, but he didn't deserve what had happened to him.

When they reached Gibbs' ATV each of them took two bottles of water. Gibbs also took the rope.

"How long has it been?" Pierce asked after they had been walking for what he thought was at least an hour.

Katie took out her phone and checked. "Forty minutes."

"You have any service?"

"Nope."

"Damn."

"Keep moving. That thing should be waking up about now and we've still got a long way to go," Gibbs told them.

"How far do you think we've come?" Katie asked.

"About two, maybe two and a half miles. We've still got at least ten more to go. That's going to take another four to five hours."

Katie moaned. "If that thing's awake and it comes after us we're never going to make it … and now it looks like it's going to rain." She was right, the sky was darkening in the west.

"We will. We just have to keep moving," Pierce assured her, even though he wasn't sure they would. They walked for another mile before they saw the next Pomoola. It was on the road in front of them. A moment later, it was joined by another one.

Blaizdell and Grant drove along the old logging road with Blaizdell in the lead. The tranquilizer rifle was slung over his shoulder. The pistol was in a holster strapped to his waist. Grant was similarly armed. Here and there the tracks of other ATVs showed that someone had recently used the road. Grant could have driven faster, but he went slowly so he could scan the woods on either side for any sign of the people he was looking for … or the creatures he hoped not to see.

For the first ten miles the ride was uneventful. Chickadees flittered in and out of the bushes that lined the road while blue jays called to each other from the tops of trees. The largest thing they came across was a red fox. Then Blaizdell thought he saw something big at the top of a rise in the road ahead, silhouetted against the darkening sky. He stopped and held up a hand for Grant to do the same.

"What is it?" Grant asked.

Blaizdell cut his engine so they could talk. "I saw something up there. It was big. It was there for a second and then it was gone."

Grant scanned the road ahead, but it was empty. "Could it

have been a moose or a bear?"

"Maybe, but I didn't get that feeling. It didn't look right. Let's go, but keep your eyes open.

Blaizdell was beginning to think his eyes had just been playing tricks on him as the ATVs neared the spot where he thought he had seen something. Maybe it was just a darker spot in the developing storm clouds. Nevertheless, his nerves were on high alert as they continued along the road.

"There they are!" Blaizdell called back to Grant when he crested the rise.

DAY 13 – 2

Pierce, Katie and Gibbs stood frozen, looking at the two Pomoola that had appeared between them and their salvation.

"What do we do now?" Katie asked, her voice cracking with emotion.

It was Gibbs who answered. "Keep going and see what they do."

Hands shaking, Pierce nocked an arrow. He wanted to be ready if the creatures attacked. The tranquilizer worked, but it was slow to take effect and it was only a single shot. There was also the pistol, but that was only good at close range. The second Pomoola could be on them by then even if Gibbs managed to get a dart into one. Pierce wasn't about to let that happen.

"Let's go," he said after he had stepped between Katie and the creatures. They hadn't taken five steps before the Pomoolas stepped off the road and disappeared into the woods. A second later they heard the sound of a gas motor. Pierce felt a huge sense of relief as the sound grew louder. A minute later, two ATVs crested the rise in front of them. The men atop them were dressed in green Maine Game Warden uniforms.

Katie grasped Pierce's arm. "Thank God," she gasped as they stood in disbelief and watched as the ATVs motored toward them.

When he stopped in front of them, the lead driver frowned at Pierce and then nodded to Gibbs. "What's going on here, Jeff? Laura said you were coming out here to get some kids and bring them back. You run into trouble?"

"Pomoolas," Gibbs answered.

The warden looked Pierce and Katie over before asking. "Weren't there supposed to be three of them out here?"

"There were. The Pomoola killed one."

When he heard that, the second game warden broke in. "Wait? What? Are you serious? This isn't some kind of joke?"

They all looked at him like he was crazy. "No joke," Gibbs finally said. "Didn't you see the two of them up there on the road just before you got here?"

"I saw something, but I couldn't tell what it was," Blaizdell answered.

"It was them," Pierce answered, pointing back the way the wardens had come. The Pomoola were back.

Blaizdell and Grant spun in their seats to look behind them. "Ah, crap," Blaizdell swore while Grant sat speechless, staring at the creatures.

"Now what?" Pierce asked.

"Now we leave. There are five of us and only two of them, and we have the tranquilizers. We shouldn't have any problems," Gibbs told him.

Grant turned to face Pierce and stared past him in horror. "Make that four. There are two more of them behind you."

Pierce spun around and saw the warden was right. Two more of the creatures were advancing up the road toward them.

"Get on!" Blaizdell yelled. "We have to get out of here"

Pierce clambered into the seat next to Blaizdell while Katie climbed onto his lap. Gibbs scrambled to join Grant on the other ATV.

"Hold on," Blaizdell warned them. Then he yanked the handlebars to the right and hit the gas. The ATV spun in a tight circle, aiming them back toward civilization. Grant did the same, and now he and Gibbs were in the lead. Then a rumble of distant thunder split the air, drowning out the angry growls of the Pomoola.

Pierce stared at the creatures in front of him who were standing their ground. The only way home was through them. A thought that he didn't relish.

"The ones behind us are coming!" Katie practically screamed in his ear.

Pierce spun around to look. One of the Pomoolas was coming toward them. Its strides were impossibly long and even though it wasn't running, it covered the ground at an alarming rate. He was about to nock an arrow when he saw the red of a tranquilizer dart appear on its chest. It stopped and looked down at the dart as if it was wondering what it was doing there before roaring and yanking it out. A second later it was advancing on them again.

By this time, Pierce was off the ATV ready to draw the bow. Adrenaline was surging through his veins. "If it doesn't stop I'm going to shoot the damn thing."

"Wait. Give it a chance to work," Blaizdell practically begged, but Pierce was having none of it. He raised the bow and drew the shaft back to his cheek. Twenty yards, fifteen, ten. At this distance it would be impossible to miss. He was ready to release the arrow when the monster stumbled and went down. As soon as it did, the second one roared. A second later it was charging toward them. Blaizdell hit it with a dart, but it had zero chance of stopping the thing before it reached them.

Peck's crushed skull flashed across Pierce's mind. There was no way he was going to let that happen to Katie. He released the arrow he had been holding in check. The Pomoola was less than ten yards away when the shaft buried itself into the creature's chest. It didn't even slow its charge. Pierce was desperately trying to nock another arrow when the monster grabbed Blaizdell and ripped him off the ATV. Pierce watched in horror as the Pomoola held the game warden in its right hand while it raised its left, the one holding a jagged rock, high above its head. Its intent was clear. In a second it was going to crush Blaizdell's skull. Then he heard Katie scream … a scream of anger, not fear.

The axe whistled past his head and bit deep into the attacking Pomoola's shoulder. Katie tried to draw the axe back, but it was ripped from her hands when the creature staggered back a step and glared at them. It tried to raise the rock, but its arm wouldn't work. It growled once and slowly dropped to the ground.

Pierce was about to help Blaizdell when a shout from the other ATV stopped him. "Help him," he told Katie, and turned to see what was happening with Gibbs and the other warden.

One of the Pomoola was down, a tranquilizer in its chest. The second monster was standing over it, glaring at the men. Pierce rushed forward so he could get a better shot if it charged. Instead, it grabbed its fallen brethren and started to drag it off into the woods.

Gibbs fired a dart at it. The dart hit it in the shoulder and then fell out. "Shit," he swore as the creature disappeared into the woods.

"Get on!" he yelled at Pierce. "We have to leave now!"

Katie was already helping Blaizdell up, but there was no way he was going to be able to drive. His shoulder was dislocated and hung at an odd angle. "Get him on. I'll drive," Pierce yelled, and jumped onto the driver's seat.

When Blaizdell was stuffed between him and Katie, Pierce spun the throttle and the ATV jumped forward, nearly knocking her off. "Slow down," she told him when he hit a bump and she was almost thrown off.

"Slow down! Blaizdell's hurt! We can't keep up!" he yelled to Gibbs and Grant as they started to open the gap between them.

Gibbs looked back, saw them falling behind and tapped Grant on the shoulder. A second later, the other ATV pulled to the side of the old road and waited for them to catch up. "Take the lead and go as fast as you can. We'll follow you," he told them when they pulled alongside. Before Pierce could pull away, a flash of lightening lit up the sky and a hard rain engulfed them. Within minutes visibility was reduced to less than a hundred feet by the storm clouds and a wall of falling water.

Pierce gave the throttle a quick twist, and the ATV's tires kicked up a shower of dirt and grass. He quickly let off on the throttle and the ATV jerked to a stop. "Idiot," he mumbled. Clamping down on the adrenaline that was rushing through him, he tried again. This time he managed to get the ATV moving smoothly. Gibbs and Grant followed once they were past. Behind them, two unconscious Pomoolas lay on the ground. One was merely unconscious. The other was dying from blood loss and the arrow in its chest.

Lightning continued to light up the sky as they fled along the old logging road. Each strike seemed closer than the last while the downpour continued to intensify. The road got so muddy and slippery that Pierce had to slow to nearly a crawl to keep from sliding off it.

"Can't you go any faster?" Katie called to him over the sound of the rain.

"Not if we want to stay on the road. I've almost lost it twice already!" he shouted back.

Another flash of lightning and crash of thunder made him flinch. That one was really close. He was still recovering from the shock of it when he had to brake for a log spanning the road. *It must have been blown down in the storm*, he thought.

Grant hit the brakes when the lead ATV came to an abrupt stop. "What the hell are they doing?" was all he had time to say before a Pomoola rushed out of the woods and yanked him off the ATV.

"Gibbs, help!" he managed to blurt out before the creature slammed him in the side of the head with a rock-like fist. Then it threw him over its shoulder and fled back into the woods. The whole thing only took a few seconds.

A shout from behind that was almost drowned out by the downpour, made Pierce turn around in his seat. Gibbs was still on the ATV behind them, but Grant was gone.

What the hell? Where is he? Before he could ask, Gibbs jumped out of the ATV and ran up to them.

"Why did you stop?" he demanded.

"There's a log across the road."

"Where the hell is Grant?" Pierce yelled back.

"A Pomoola ran out of the woods and grabbed him when we stopped. We have to keep going."

"How? There's a log in the road."

"Go around it. We can't stay here."

"What about Grant?"

"He's gone. We can't help him. We need to go, now! Blaizdell, come with me, it'll be faster."

Katie hopped out of the ATV they were on and let Blaizdell get off. Once he was, she scrambled back on next to Pierce. "Go," she said as soon as she was there.

The way around the log wasn't difficult. The rain made it slippery, but the ground was firm and flat. It was obvious the log had been placed there to slow them down and it had done just that. Pierce wouldn't stop for another one.

As soon as Pierce was back on the logging road, he gave the ATV more gas. In just seconds he was going faster than he had dared before. There were no complaints from Katie as she held on. "I wish this thing had seat belts," was all she said after she bounced three inches off the seat after one particularly vicious bump.

Pierce thought they were in the clear after they had gone another mile without any sign of the Pomoolas. That changed when he rounded a curve and saw two of the creatures standing in the road a hundred yards ahead of them. He braked to a stop and waited for Gibbs and Blaizdell to catch up. Pierce was out of the ATV with an arrow nocked and ready when they pulled up behind him a minute later.

"I wish you guys would have brought a gun instead of those things," he told Gibbs when the man joined him.

"Yeah, me too." Gibbs admitted.

The blow to his head didn't knock Grant out but it stunned him. By the time he was able to fight back the Pomoola was far from the road. He was lying over the creature backward, his face buried in wet, coarse hair which smelled like a dog that had rolled in something dead. It took a minute to gather his wits, then he tried to kick his legs and pound the monster's back with his fists. He didn't hurt it, but it got its attention because it threw him to the ground. He hit with such force that his right forearm snapped in a compound fracture. Pieces of jagged bone broke through the skin and he screamed in pain.

The Pomoola stared down at him from what appeared an impossible height. Then it reached down, took his head in both its massive hands … and twisted.

DAY 13 – 3

Pierce jumped out of the ATV and grabbed his bow. "Check behind us. They seem to attack in pairs."

Katie glanced behind them. The road was clear … and then it wasn't. One of the monsters seemed to materialize out of the woods right in front of her eyes. "There's one back here, too."

"Keep your eyes on it. Tell me if it gets any closer. I'm going after the two up there," Gibbs told them.

Pierce couldn't believe what he was hearing. "What? Are you crazy?"

"It's the only way. I'll try and tranq one with this," he said, holding up the rifle. Then he slapped the pistol, "And the other one with this. Then I'm going to run like hell to get back here. You cover me with the bow. Shoot them if they come after me."

"What about the one back there?" Katie asked.

Gibbs handed her the other rifle. "That one's yours. Don't shoot it until you're sure you can hit it. You'll only have one shot."

She looked doubtfully at the rifle, but she took it.

"Hey, I'm here too, you know," Blaizdell said. He had tucked the dislocated arm in his shirt and was holding a tranquilizer pistol in his other hand.

"Okay, do it," Pierce agreed.

When Gibbs started walking toward the Pomoolas, one of them started coming toward him. After ten feet or so, it stopped, drew itself to its full height and roared at him. When Gibbs failed to stop, it came another ten feet forward, stopped, and roared again.

When the Pomoola threw back his head to roar at him a

second time, Gibbs raised the rifle, aimed and pulled the trigger. With a puff of gas, the tranquilizer dart sped toward the creature and buried itself in its chest. As soon as he saw it hit, Gibbs turned and ran back toward Pierce. The Pomoola roared again, then charged. The second one was close behind it.

Behind them, Katie yelled and raised her rifle. "It's coming!" She and Blaizdell fired at the same time. One dart hit the Pomoola in the chest, the other in the face. Even after both darts hit, it didn't stop. It didn't even slow down.

Pierce spun and drew to shoot at the charging Pomoola, but Blaizdell was in the way. "Get down!" he yelled. Blaizdell dropped, but, in the time it took for him to react, the creature halved the distance between them.

Pierce let the arrow fly. It struck the Pomoola in the throat. He was trying to nock his last hunting arrow when the monster reached out to grab Katie. The monster was inches from her when Blaizdell threw himself into it. It swatted the man away like he was a child. Before it could reach for Katie again, Pierce was attacking it with his hunting knife. He slashed it once across the face before one of its arms caught him in the side and sent him flying. The monster then stepped back, tried to roar, and collapsed.

Pierce was staring at the fallen creature when Gibbs grabbed him by the shoulder. "Get ready, the other one's coming."

They all turned to look. The creature with the dart in its chest was lumbering toward them through the rain. The second was close behind. The tranquilizer was working, but would it take effect in time? Pierce took a chance the tranquilizer would drop it and shifted his attention to the second one. He was about to draw and fire when the first Pomoola pitched forward, not five feet from them. Two down, one to go. The remaining Pomoola stopped its charge and glared at them.

Gibbs reloaded Katie and Blaizdell's tranquilizers and handed them back to them before reloading his own. When they were all rearmed, he turned back to face the last Pomoola. "You ready?" he asked Pierce.

Pierce nodded in reply.

Gibbs started forward. Before he went five steps Katie

moved forward to join him, pistol in hand. Pierce tried to stop her, but she was having none of it. "If we both shoot it, it'll go down faster. Then we can get the hell out of here."

"Then I'm coming with you," Pierce told her.

When they stepped around the fallen Pomoola, the remaining creature growled at them once, and then disappeared into the woods.

"Hurry, we have to leave before these wake up or that one comes back with reinforcements," Gibbs said.

Pierce looked at him in amazement. "Why don't we just kill the damn things so they can't follow us?"

Gibbs just shook his head. "No time. We need to get out of here."

Katie and Pierce got back in the lead ATV while Gibbs and Blaizdell climbed into the second one. A minute later they were driving around the unconscious Pomoola and heading toward the road.

When they crested a small rise Pierce saw the locked gate in front of them. "We're going to make it," he said, excitement and relief in his voice.

Katie was less sure. "I'll believe it when we're out of here and back at the motel."

Behind them, Gibbs yelled to them when he saw the gate. "Get to my truck. Leave the ATV."

That sounded good to Pierce. He stopped just in front of the gate and he and Katie scrambled over it. A minute later Gibbs maneuvered the ATV he was driving around the gate and pulled to a stop next to his pickup. He jumped off, reached in his pocket, dug out his keys and tossed them to Pierce, "Here, take it and leave. We'll follow in Blaizdell's truck. Go to the museum."

Pierce snatched the keys out of the air. "What museum?"

"Never mind, I know," Katie told him, and pushed him toward the pickup.

After they were in the truck he glanced in the rearview mirror. Gibbs was helping Blaizdell into what must have been the warden's pickup.

"Go!" Katie shook him and yelled when he just sat there

watching Gibbs and Blaizdell.

She didn't have to tell him twice. He started the pickup and searched for the wiper switch. Once they were sweeping the rain from the windshield he shifted into first and stomped on the gas. The tires spit gravel as they spun on the loose dirt of the shoulder and then left a trail of rubber when they hit the pavement.

"Where's this museum?" Pierce asked once they were on the road and moving.

Katie gave him directions. Except for that they rode in silence, each trying to deal with the ordeal they had just been through. "There it is," she told him when she saw it ahead on the right.

Pierce pulled over, parked in front of it, and waited for Gibbs to pull in behind them. They weren't there for more than a minute before Laura Hickman opened the door of the museum and rushed out to meet them.

"Come inside," she told them when Gibbs and Blaizdell joined them.

Once they were all in the museum, Laura hovered over them like a mother hen. "What happened? Why are there only four of you?"

Gibbs gave her a warning look and shook his head. "Pomoolas. We can talk about it in the morning. Right now I need to take Blaizdell to the hospital to get his shoulder taken care of."

Pierce looked incredulous. "Tomorrow? We can't wait until tomorrow. What about Grant? He's still out there."

"Grant is ... gone. We couldn't do anything tonight anyway. Are you willing to go out there in the rain and the dark and face those things again?"

Pierce looked at Katie. She shook her head "no" and he reluctantly agreed.

"All right, you two go back to the motel, clean up and get a good night's sleep. We'll meet back here tomorrow morning at nine. Then we can talk about what we're going to do. In the meantime, don't talk to anyone about this. And stay off the internet."

When Pierce and Katie stepped outside, the rain had tapered off to a light drizzle. They were already soaked to the skin so they just walked to the motel. When Pierce followed Katie into the room it looked like heaven to him. A queen-sized bed, a desk and chair, an easy chair and a flat screen TV had never looked so good. He wanted to flop down on the bed but didn't dare. Not in the wet, muddy clothes he was wearing. Katie didn't look much better, but at least she had dry clothes to change into. All he had was what he was wearing.

"I'll shower first and change. Then I'll wash your clothes while you clean up."

While Katie was in the shower, Pierce stripped off his wet clothes and wrapped himself in a blanket from the bed. Then he turned the TV on and cycled through the channels looking for something to watch. After what he had just been through, everything struck him as useless and banal. He was struggling through a news show on CNN when Katie emerged from the bathroom wearing just a towel.

"Your turn," she told him.

He stood up and tossed the blanket on the bed. "Ew," she said when she saw he was getting aroused. "Not on your life. Get in that shower. I'll be back later."

He had to agree with her "ew" when he got a look at himself in the mirror. *Christ, I'm a mess.* He couldn't blame her for her reaction. He looked terrible. His unshaven face sported a scruffy, uneven mess of whiskers that could hardly be called a beard, his hair was unkempt and greasy, and his face and hands were smudged with dirt. He also looked a lot skinnier than he had the last time he had seen himself in a mirror.

He climbed in the shower and found it filled with Katie's scented body wash, shampoo, conditioner, a lady's pink razor and shaving cream. *What the hell?* he thought and grabbed the shampoo. After shampooing his hair twice, applying conditioner for the first time in his life and scrubbing himself all over with some pink scrubby thing, he stood under the hot water just to let it caress his aching muscles.

The room was filled with steam and the mirror covered

in condensation when he finally stepped out of the shower. He opened the bathroom door and stepped out into the room to towel off. The air-conditioned air rose goosebumps on his exposed skin. When he tired of waiting for the mirror to clear, he wiped it with the towel and set about getting rid of his unwanted facial hair. After the first scrape, that's all he could call it, with Katie's razor, he almost gave up on that idea. *What the hell did she do to this thing? It's like shaving with the lid off a rusty tin can.*

Katie breezed into the room an hour later with a large shopping bag, a pizza box and a quart bottle of coke. She dropped the bag on the bed and the pizza and soda on the desk. "I got you some new clothes and a toothbrush. Your old ones were beyond help."

Pierce eyed the clothes, but then went straight for the pizza. Katie jumped between him and the box. "Oh, no you don't. Dress first, eat second."

"But I'm famished?"

"Me too. But get dressed."

"Where are my clothes?"

"In the bag."

Katie opened the soda while Pierce dug through the bag for his new clothes. He found a pair of jeans, two t-shirts, a three-pack of socks and three pairs of black jockey shorts. "Black? Why black? Didn't they have white?"

Katie grinned at him. "White's blah. Black's sexy."

Pierce shook his head and got dressed. Then they dug into the pizza.

"I would have gotten wine, but I'm still a month away from being legal," she told him.

When Pierce reached for the last piece of pizza, Katie slapped his hand. "Hey, I'm here too you know. I've only had two pieces."

Pierce drew his hand back and stared longingly at the last piece. "I could use another one of those and a bottle of wine."

"We can call out for another pizza, but you'd have to go for the wine. We can have them bring soda. I want to be sober for tomorrow ... and tonight."

"You'll have to call. I don't have a phone," Pierce told her.

"No problem. There's only one place in town. The number's in the book over there. That's where I got this one."

"Twenty minutes," she told him after she hung up.

"Maybe we could …" he started to say, but a loud knock on the door interrupted him.

Pierce looked at Katie as if to say "*Who could that be?*"

She shrugged and shook her head.

Pierce opened the door and was surprised to see Derick Stanley. "Derick, what the hell are you doing here?"

"Where's Mike?" Stanley demanded. "If you're back, he should be too."

Pierce only hesitated for a minute before answering. "How the hell should I know? The last time I saw that asshole he was dressed up in a Bigfoot costume. I almost shot his ass until he took his mask off. Then he took off cursing. That was the last I saw him."

"When was that?"

"Two days ago."

"He was supposed to be back two days ago. He never showed up."

"Not my problem." Pierce told him and shut the door in his face.

When he turned back to Katie, she was sitting on the bed with a horrified look on her face. "God, I forgot all about Peck. What are we going to do about him?"

Pierce came and sat next to her on the bed. "I don't know. But I wasn't about to tell him he was dead and we sank him in the lake. We'll ask Gibbs in the morning."

When the pizza and cokes came twenty minutes later, they had both lost their appetites … for food at least. After a bout of frantic lovemaking they fell asleep snuggled together.

For the first night in weeks, Pierce slept in a soft bed. Better yet, he didn't have to dream about Katie, she was there, in his arms.

What the hell is going on out there? Stanley had thought when he arrived at the old logging road. The three pickups with their empty trailers were still parked on the side of the road with no sign of the ATVs or their drivers. Peck still wasn't back and there was no sign of him either. He considered hiking in, but quickly gave up on that idea. *It's too damn far and who knows what's happening. Maybe someone's growing marijuana and they're all dead. I'll wait one more day. If no one's back by tomorrow, I'm making an anonymous call to the state police.*

With nothing else to do, he went back to the motel to watch TV and surf the net. He logged onto Peck's Facebook page using Peck's computer and made up a few entries to keep things going.

Chambers is still out there, but things must be getting harder. We're supposed to get thunderstorms tonight, but he doesn't know that. I can't imagine sitting under a tarp in the dark with rain pouring down all around me. Enjoy the rain, Chambers.

He made two more trips to the old logging road. One in the afternoon, one in the evening. On the last one, things had changed, two of the pickups were gone. The only one left belonged to one of the game wardens. But now there were two ATVs sitting there in the rain.

What the hell? Why would they leave the ATVs? Something's not right here.

When he got back to the motel, he saw light around the curtain in Chambers' girlfriend's window. *She must be back. Now I'll find out what's happening and where Mike is.*

After parking in front of his room he walked over to hers and pounded on the door. *I'm going to get some answers out of her whether she likes it or not.* He was prepared to barge in and confront her when Chambers opened the door. All thoughts of barging in to her room evaporated. He did manage to demand to know where Peck was. When Chambers answered, "How the hell should I know? The last time I saw that asshole he was dressed up in a Bigfoot costume. I almost shot his ass until he took his mask off. Then he took off cursing. That was the last I saw him," he almost choked. Chambers knew what they had been doing. When he slammed the door in his face, he retreated to his own room.

After the docs at the ER put Blaizdell's shoulder back in place, he and Gibbs went back to the logging road to retrieve the ATVs. Blaizdell wasn't much help loading them, but he could still drive.

"What are we going to do about Grant's pickup?" Blaizdell asked while Gibbs was loading the ATVs.

"I don't know? Do you have a spare key for it?"

"No."

"I guess we'll have to cross that bridge when we get to it. Maybe no one has seen it parked out here."

"I doubt it. There was a young guy out here when we came. He was waiting for his buddy. He might have come back. I guess we can tell him we found him."

"Damn," Gibbs swore and shook his head. "Not really. Chambers wasn't his buddy. The Pomoolas got the one he was looking for."

"Ah, Christ. Now what are we going to do? Covering up for Grant is going to be hard enough. How are we going to explain the kid?"

"I don't know. We'll have to figure something out."

"Keeping this secret is getting harder and harder. Maybe it's time to let the cat out of the bag."

Gibbs gave him a hard look. "Are you serious? You know what would happen if we did. All hell would break loose up here. The town would never be the same. People would come up here to find them, some of them would die, and the Pomoola would be gone in a year."

"Well, this time it might not be possible to keep it quiet. Too many outsiders are involved."

DAY 14

Katie woke before Pierce. She lay in bed listening to him breathe for ten minutes before she slipped out from under the covers and headed for the bathroom. Once there, she peed and then stepped into the shower. She wanted to be showered and dressed before Pierce woke up if she could. He probably needed the sleep.

Once she was out of the shower she decided to skip brushing her teeth and blow drying her hair. She could do those later. Instead, she went back into the room, quickly dressed, and was ready to slip out the door when Pierce rolled over and opened his eyes.

"Where are you going?"

"To get coffee and breakfast. Get dressed while I'm gone. We need to be at the museum in an hour."

"Okay," he answered, and swung his legs from under the covers. When he started to stand up, Katie quickly turned away. She didn't want to see him naked. Not this morning. They had things to do.

When she came back she had two large coffees, and three egg, bacon and cheese sandwiches. Two of the sandwiches were for Pierce. He was done with both of his and staring at hers before she had managed to eat half of it. "You want the rest of this?" she asked, holding it out to him.

"No," he answered, but she knew he did.

"Take it, you pig. We have time. We'll get more."

"Nah, I'll just have some of that pizza we didn't eat last night."

"Don't you dare. It's probably gone bad by now."

"Hah. Next-day pizza was a staple back in the frat house. It'll be fine," he told her and reached for the box.

"If you eat that, you won't be kissing these lips. It's up to you."

Pierce looked between her and the pizza, shrugged, and put the piece back in the box.

"Smart man. Now let's go."

Pierce stood behind Katie as she knocked on the door of the Bigfoot Museum.

"Come in, quickly," Laura Hickman said when she opened the door.

Katie was through it in a second. Pierce hesitated a minute before following her inside. He flinched when he caught sight of the Bigfoot statue out of the corner of his eye. Along with Laura Hickman, Gibbs and Blaizdell were waiting for them. Blaizdell's arm was in a sling, but otherwise he was unscathed. A table and several folding chairs had been set up along with a pot of coffee.

"Have a seat. We need to talk," Laura Hickman told them.

Pierce was confused. What else was there to do than call the police and he said so.

"That's not a good idea," Ms. Hickman told them.

"What? You have to," Katie blurted out.

"Wait, hear me out." Laura told her.

"Two men are missing. You," she said looking at Pierce, "were the only other one out there in the woods when one of them disappeared. The other went missing trying to find you and your girlfriend. What do you think will happen if you tell them Bigfoot did it? You're the one who'll come under suspicion."

"But he didn't do anything. The Bigfoot or Pomoola, or whatever you call them, did this. You saw them," she said, looking at Gibbs and Blaizdell.

Gibbs shrugged. "Right, and if we back you up they'll think we were all in on it together. And, we have no proof. The rain will have washed away any tracks and no one will find the Pomoola if they don't want to be found. Peck is in the lake and I don't think we'll ever find Grant. The best thing we can do is all agree on a story that has nothing to do with the Pomoola."

"What kind of story could we come up with that anyone would believe? It sounds like they'll still suspect me," Pierce told them.

"Not necessarily," Blaizdell chimed in. "We have quite a marijuana problem up here. Growers stake out a territory and can be pretty brutal. That's why we post the area No Trespassing. That's what we'll say happened to your friend and Grant."

Pierce wasn't happy about it, but had to agree it might work and it was better than trying to convince people that the Bigfoot were real.

It took two hours for them to create their story, and another two to go over it and smooth it out. By the time they were done Pierce and Katie felt comfortable enough with it that they were willing to go along with it.

"Who are you going to call?" Katie asked when they were about to leave.

"Sheriff Booth, he's a friend of mine," Laura Hickman told them.

"Does he know about … them?"

"Of course, dear. He's the sheriff."

"How many times has this happened?" Pierce asked.

Laura Hickman glanced at Gibbs before answering. When he nodded, she said, "Every once in a while a cow will go missing, but people … no."

"I can't believe people don't just jump that fence and go out there anyway," Pierce told her.

"People around here know to stay out of there."

"But what about outsiders like us?"

"We don't get too many of those. Now, why don't you two go back to your motel? I'm sure Sheriff Booth will want to talk to you after we tell him what happened."

"But …" Pierce started to say, and then Katie grabbed his arm and dragged him toward the door.

"I think that's a good idea. We'll wait for him there," she told them.

Pierce turned to her once they were outside. "Why did you drag me out?"

"Because they obviously have a plan. They've known about the Pomoola for a long time. They've been protecting them and keeping their existence a secret. Nothing we say is going to make a difference. If you make a big deal of it, they'll do what they have to, to keep that secret. Even if it means feeding you to the lions."

Pierce was quiet. Then he shook his head. "You really think so?"

"Yes. Now let's go back to the room and wait for the sheriff."

While they waited, Katie drilled Pierce on what he was going to say. He went over the story they had all agreed on. It proved to be unnecessary. When Sheriff Booth arrived he repeated the story back to them and asked if they agreed with everything. When they said yes, he told them they were free to leave. From the way he said it, they both knew it was more than a suggestion.

As Katie gathered her stuff and packed, Pierce moved the shades aside and looked out the window. Sheriff Booth's cruiser was still parked outside. "The sheriff is here, but I don't see him. You think he's waiting to see if we leave?"

"I don't know, but let's make him happy if he is. I'm almost ready."

On the way to her car, Katie elbowed Pierce in the side. "There he is, in Stanley's room. He must be telling him what happened."

They couldn't hear what Booth was saying, but he was pointing toward the window. Stanley was sitting on the bed with a stunned look on his face.

Katie handed him her suitcase and the keys to the car. "Pick me up at the office. I'm going to check out and pay the bill."

"You should let me do that."

"Forget it. You can pay for lunch and dinner, and tonight's room."

"All right," he agreed. "I'll meet you out front."

While he waited for her, he kept an eye on the police cruiser in the rearview mirror. Sherriff Booth came out of Stanley's room just as Katie was coming out of the office. Booth stopped and watched as Katie got in the passenger side. Apparently satisfied they were leaving, he made his way to the cruiser.

"I don't believe this. What do you think he told Stanley?"

"The same thing he told us. Go. I don't think any of them want us around. And that's okay with me. I never want to come back here again."

Stanley had a bad feeling when he saw the police cruiser park outside. He was waiting for a knock on the door. When it didn't come he stepped outside to see what was going on. He was just in time to see the sheriff disappear into the room Chambers and the girl were in. Fifteen minutes later, there had been a knock on his door.

What do I do? The sheriff suggested I go home. I should stick around and see what happened to Mike, but who's going to pay for the room? I sure as hell can't and it's on my card. He was going to pay me back. What happens now?

He glanced at the clock on the bedside stand and realized he only had fifteen minutes to decide. If he didn't check out by then, he was going to be charged for another day. *Fuck it. He said he'd call me when they knew more. There's nothing I can do here. I'm going home.*

Gibbs and Blaizdell rode together on Blaizdell's ATV. Blaizdell drove with a tranquilizer pistol in a holster strapped to his chest. Gibbs rode next to him, armed with a twelve gauge shotgun with a six-shell magazine loaded with buckshot. He also had the tranquilizer rifle. If they saw a Pomoola he'd try to scare it off with the shotgun or tranq it. He'd shoot to kill only as a last resort.

"Where's the one those kids killed? It should have been right here" Blaizdell asked when they reached the spot where Pierce and Katie had been attacked.

"Maybe it wasn't dead, or the others dragged it away. Either way, it's gone."

"Your ATV is right up there. Any sign of them?" Blaizdell asked as he drove the ATV.

"No. Can't you go any faster?"

"Not with one arm. Just keep your eyes open."

"Stop!" Gibbs commanded.

"What?"

"I saw something in the woods. Something big."

Blaizdell brought the ATV to a stop and peered into the woods where Gibbs was pointing. He only saw the Pomoola in front of them emerge from the woods from the corner of his eye. "There! There's one of them in front of us."

When Gibbs turned to look at it, the one he had glimpsed ran out of the woods toward them. There was no time for the tranquilizer, so he fired the shotgun into the air. The Pomoola abruptly stopped, as if not sure what to do. Gibbs was leveling the shotgun at it when Blaizdell shot it with his pistol. The dart hit the creature in the arm. It pulled it out and roared at them, but didn't charge. They were in a stalemate until the Pomoola wobbled and fell to the ground.

"Here comes the other one!" Blaizdell yelled and Gibbs turned to face it.

"It's too close for a dart. I have to shoot it," he told Blaizdell. Then he raised the shotgun and pulled the trigger. The explosion from the gun split the silence and the Pomoola dropped.

"Did you kill it?"

"I don't know. Drive around it, but don't get too close. I'll hit it with a dart as we go by."

"You're going to have to hook up the cable. I'm no good with this arm. Just keep the shotgun ready."

Gibbs helped Blaizdell turn the ATV around and then hooked the tow cable to the front of his damaged ATV. "Go," he said when he was ready.

Blaizdell took up the slack on the cable until he felt the drag of Gibbs' ATV. "Here we go."

They made it back to the trucks without seeing another Pomoola. "Now what?" Blaizdell asked.

"Now we load these up and get out of here. That just leaves Peck's ATV and both camps. The sheriff and I will come out here tomorrow to clean up the rest of this mess."

"You ready to do this?" the sheriff asked Gibbs as they prepared to drive around the gate blocking access to the old logging road. Gibbs, armed the same way today that he had been the day before, nodded.

Booth maneuvered the ATV around the gate and they were on their way. "This is where I shot the Pomoola," Gibbs said when they reached the spot. The only sign that anything had happened there was an empty twelve gauge shotgun shell. "Stop and I'll grab that."

The next thing they ran into was Peck's ATV. "It's a mess," Gibbs said. "We're going to have to use the winch to get it back on its wheels before we can tow it out."

Booth shook his head. "We can't move it yet. It's a crime scene. Let's go on."

"Take this turnoff," Gibbs said when they reached the side trail to Peck's campsite.

Gibbs knew what to expect so the extent of the carnage didn't surprise him. Booth, on the other hand did not. "The Pomoola did this? It looks like a bear could have done this."

"Sure does," Gibbs agreed.

Booth snapped a dozen pictures before they got back on the ATV and headed toward Pierce's camp.

"This is where it gets hairy. If they're coming after us, this is where it's going to happen," Gibbs said. "We're going to be weaving in and out of trees and our line of sight is going to be pretty short. I'll have to use the shotgun if we're attacked. Keep your gun ready too."

"What do you want to do with this?" Gibbs asked when they reached Pierce's campsite.

"Take it down and pack it up. Don't leave anything. I'll stand guard while you do that."

"Right," Gibbs answered. "Keep your eye on that ridge up there. That's where they watched us from. The damn things can jump right off it," he said as he started to dismantle the campsite.

After he loaded the last piece of gear onto the ATV, Gibbs glanced around the site to see if he had missed anything. "You want me to get rid of the stones from the fire pit?"

"Yeah, that's a good idea. Do what you can to scatter the ashes and spare firewood too."

Booth maneuvered the ATV out of the woods and onto the old logging road and breathed a sigh of relief. "Whew, I'm glad we're out from under those trees and back where we can see what's ahead of us."

"I don't think you have to worry about them. I think they're gone," Gibbs told him.

"Gone? Gone where?"

"I don't know, but they're gone. The woods seem ... normal. I've seen a few squirrels, heard some birds and just don't feel the same tension I did when they were around. We'll keep our eyes open and stay ready on the way back, but I definitely think they're gone."

"God, I hope you're right. I'll feel a lot better bringing a search party out here to look for Grant and that Peck kid if they are."

They made it back to Gibbs' truck without any sign of the Pomoola.

"Have you heard *anything* yet?" Katie asked when Pierce met her after work.

"Yeah. I got a call from Sheriff Booth today. He said there was no sign of Peck or Grant. They're blaming the whole thing on drugs. He also said they cleaned up my campsite and that I can come and get all the gear anytime I want."

"You're not going, are you?"

"Hell no. I told him to keep it or get rid of it. I want no part of it or Tinkers Falls."

"So that's it?"

"As far as I'm concerned it is. What about you?"

"Oh, yeah. The townspeople can keep their secret. Someday it's bound to come out, but I'm not going to be the one to open that box. Who knows what Gibbs and the rest would do if we did."

About the Author

Dan Foley is an ex-plumber, ex-Navy Nuke, Ex-Senior Reactor Operator and ex-Nuclear Operations Specialist. He has lived on the east coast, the west coast, and places in between. Dan attributes his dark sense of humor on growing up in his home state of New Jersey and then serving on nuclear submarines. He currently resides in Connecticut.

Bibliography

Abandoned
Death's Companion
Gypsy
Intruder
Reunion
The Whispers of Crows
Wolf's Tale

Curious about other Crossroad Press books?
Stop by our site:
http://www.crossroadpress.com
We offer quality writing
in digital, audio, and print formats.